## "From now on, we make all decisions together."

"What about when we can't agree?" Which, Torey estimated, would be about 90 percent of the time.

From the look on Patrick's face, he knew that, too. "How about we let Ruby be the tiebreaker? Unless you think it would stress her out too much."

Torey considered. "I think she'd like being involved." Maybe a little too much. "I'll ask her about it." She hesitated, as something occurred to her. "Although…getting Ruby in the middle of this might cause a different problem."

"What kind of problem?"

Torey didn't want to mention this—she really didn't. But she'd probably better. Ruby had all the subtlety of a wrecking ball. "I think she's got a nutty idea in her head. She's determined to see all of us kids matched up and settled down, and I'm next in line."

"That so?" Patrick rose and started toward the door. "She got somebody in mind for you?"

He still wasn't getting it. Torey sucked in a steadying breath. "You."

**Laurel Blount** lives on a small farm in Georgia with her husband, David, their four children, a milk cow, dairy goats, assorted chickens, an enormous dog, three spoiled cats and one extremely bossy goose with boundary issues. She divides her time between farm chores, homeschooling and writing, and she's happiest with a cup of steaming tea at her elbow and a good book in her hand.

### Books by Laurel Blount

### Love Inspired

Visit the Author Profile page at LoveInspired.com.

# A Family to Foster

## Laurel Blount

## LOVE INSPIRED
INSPIRATIONAL ROMANCE

# LOVE INSPIRED®

## INSPIRATIONAL ROMANCE

Recycling programs for this product may not exist in your area.

ISBN-13: 978-1-335-59832-5

A Family to Foster

Love Inspired
22 Adelaide St. West, 41st Floor
Toronto, Ontario M5H 4E3, Canada
www.LoveInspired.com

**Printed in U.S.A.**

The just man walketh in his integrity:
his children are blessed after him.
—*Proverbs* 20:7

To our son-in-love Kevin Brock,
a man of integrity, kindness and strength.
You have blessed our family beyond measure.

# Chapter One

"Is Joshie in trouble again?"

"I don't know, Jillybean." As they walked into Cedar Ridge Middle School, Patrick Callahan looked down at his five-year-old foster daughter—and winced.

Those ponytails were really lopsided today. Jill and her older brother, Josh, had been with him four months, but he was still flunking little girl hairdos. He'd watch some more YouTube videos and see if he couldn't up his game.

It was the least he could do. These two had already been failed by too many adults. The details their social worker had shared about their past had made Patrick sick to his stomach.

But not surprised. He was a Callahan. Most of his cousins had done stints in foster care before moving on to various Georgia prisons. He knew more about the darker side of family life than most people. He also knew how much difference even one halfway decent adult could make in a kid's life.

That's why he'd signed up for this job in the first place.

He gave Jill's hand a reassuring squeeze as they walked down a hallway decorated with scarecrows and bright fall leaves. Outside, the trees covering the north Georgia mountains had barely started to shift color, but fall had arrived at the school two weeks ago when the calendar had flipped to September.

He paused outside the wooden door marked Principal and squatted to look Jill in the eye.

"Sweetie, Mrs. Edwards will probably want to talk to me alone. You can sit with the secretary until we're done, okay?" He should've brought a book or a toy to keep her occupied. Another parenting demerit.

Jill nodded—and wiped her running nose on her pink shirtsleeve. He should've brought along some tissues, too. Those demerits were adding up.

Jill had stayed home from kindergarten with a cold, the first time one of the kids had been sick on his watch. He'd set an alarm to remind him when she needed her medicine, he had the pediatrician on speed dial, and he'd bought enough chicken noodle soup and saltine crackers to feed an army.

He'd had her set up nice and cozy in his office at Callahan's Motors. She'd been snuggled under a blanket, watching cartoons and drinking juice while he rebuilt a client's '49 Mercury. Then the school had called about Josh.

Again.

Inside the office, Betty Johnson, the school's gray-haired secretary was typing on her computer.

"Joshie!"

Josh was slumped on a bench against the wall. The twelve-year-old looked up as Patrick approached, then refocused his gaze on his sneakers, his cheeks mottling red.

Jill ran to her brother, worming her way under his arm to nestle against his skinny chest. Josh's expression didn't change, but the boy's arm went around his sister protectively.

"Hey, Josh," Patrick said quietly. "What's going on?"

"I hate this school," the boy muttered. "That's what's going on."

Alicia Edwards poked her head out of her office. "There you are. Thanks for coming in. Betty will keep an eye on Josh while we talk, and I see we've got Jill, too?" A question lilted in the veteran principal's voice.

"She stayed home sick," Patrick explained. "Sorry, but it was such short notice—"

"That's fine. She can wait with her brother." The principal beckoned.

Hastily, Patrick plucked several tissues from a handy box. "Wipe your nose with these," he murmured to Jill. "Not your sleeve, okay?" Then he walked into the office and his heart sank.

This was worse than he'd thought.

Mitzi Crawford, the middle-aged social worker who'd recently taken over Josh and Jill's case, sat perched in one of two maroon armchairs. She glanced up as Patrick came in, her heavy perfume hanging in the air like a threat.

Mitzi couldn't seem to get past the fact that Patrick was a Callahan—a name more often seen on Cedar Ridge police reports than its foster parent rolls. He suspected she was looking for an excuse to move the kids out of his home. He hoped Josh hadn't just handed that excuse to her.

"Have a seat." Principal Edwards settled behind her desk.

"Thanks." Patrick sat on the edge of the armchair, hoping he wouldn't get any grease on the upholstery. He should've changed clothes, but the call had sounded urgent. "So," he said, "Somebody going to tell me what this is all about?"

*Please, Lord. Let it be something minor.*

For a few seconds nobody spoke. Then Principal Edwards cleared her throat. "Josh has been suspended."

"*What?* Why?"

"He used one of the library's computers to hack into the school's administrative database and make some…unauthorized changes."

Frustration, well laced with panic, rose up in Patrick's chest. Josh was a whiz with electronics. When the television had gone wonky after a thunderstorm, he'd had it fixed before Patrick could get off the couch.

He'd also bypassed the kid-protecting limits Patrick had painstakingly installed on his computer at home, not once but three times.

He swallowed. "What kind of changes?"

The principal slipped on a pair of glasses and tapped on her laptop. "He changed the lunch menus, switched up his schedule, and tweaked the school calendar. Apparently, we're having pizza for lunch for the foreseeable future, he's no longer taking English, and our school has Fridays off from now until…forever. Oh. And our school mascot was changed from a tiger to a…" She squinted and turned her computer in his direction. "What would you say this is?"

Patrick leaned forward to examine the screen. Oh, boy. "It looks like a possum." He cleared his throat. "That's—I'm sorry this happened. How much trouble is he in?"

"He's *suspended*," Mitzi said sharply. "How much trouble do you think he's in?"

"Suspension may seem severe." Mrs. Edwards slipped off her glasses. "But confidential records are in this system. An adult hacker would face criminal charges, and this is the fifth time Josh has been in trouble since school started. Normally, we have a three-strike policy, but I extended that because I knew he'd been moved to a new foster placement over the summer. That's also why I asked Miss Crawford to join us today." She paused. "How's Josh adjusting?"

Mitzi snorted.

"I'm still working to connect with him," Patrick admitted. "We'll get there, but it's taking some time."

"I see." Mrs. Edwards sighed. "Well, I'm sorry to add to your troubles, but Josh will be put on home instruction for a week. When he returns, he'll serve an additional week of in-school suspension."

"I understand." Patrick didn't know what he'd do with Josh at home for a week. He'd have to come to the garage—no way could the kid be left unsupervised. Josh wasn't going like that. "I'll... talk to him."

"Thank you." Principal Edwards sent him a sympathetic smile. "Josh is obviously a smart young man. Our computer science teacher still hasn't figured out how he pulled this off. However, it's unacceptable behavior, and we all need to make that clear." She turned to the social worker. "Do you have any suggestions, Miss Crawford?"

"I certainly do," Mitzi said ominously. "I'd like to speak to Patrick alone, please."

Mrs. Edwards raised an eyebrow, but she nodded. "Of course."

After the principal left the room, Mitzi shifted in her chair and frowned at him. "This placement isn't working out. I'm starting the process to remove the children from your home."

"But it's only been a few months—"

"Sometimes that's long enough. You heard what the principal said. This is criminal behavior. Josh is headed down the wrong path, and I hardly think you're the right person to stop him."

Heat crept up Patrick's jaw. He'd learned not to dodge digs about his family, so he met her gaze squarely.

"I'm a Callahan in name only, Mitzi. Check your records. I passed the background check with flying colors."

Mitzi didn't blink. "I know that. I also know that before you cut a deal with the police, you were helping your father take apart the cars your cousins stole."

"Because I didn't know they were stolen."

Mitzi shrugged. "So you say. Your cousins said otherwise, I'm told. These children need a strong, positive role model. In all honesty, I'm not sure someone with your family history should've been approved to foster in the first place, and I've said as much to my supervisor. Not," she added irritably, "that she's paid any attention. Hopefully, after today that will change."

Patrick sent up a short, desperate prayer. *Help me not to lose my temper, Lord.* In fairness, Mitzi was only saying to his face what people had said behind his back for years.

"My cousins were mad because I went to the police when I found out they'd turned my dad's garage into a chop shop. And Mrs. Darnell isn't listening because the county doesn't have enough qualified foster parents. They definitely don't have many willing to take on a sibling group including a kid with challenges like Josh has. His behavior is why their last foster family asked them to be removed, remember? And the family before that. You people can't just keep shuffling these poor kids around."

"We're not going to," Mitzi informed him. "The decision has been made to terminate parental rights. Adoption is their new case plan." She shrugged. "For Jill, anyway."

"What do you mean? What about Josh?"

"Like you said, his behavioral problems make him a much harder placement. Plus, he's a boy— adoptive parents prefer girls." Her phone chirped, and Mitzi dug in her bag until she found it. "And he's older, and everybody wants young kids. His prospects just aren't very good." She frowned at her phone.

"So—what?" Patrick dug his fingers into his

knees to keep from grabbing Mitzi's phone and flinging it against the wall. "You're going to throw him away like a piece of garbage?"

"Of course not," she said without looking up. "He'll be taken care of. I'm checking into a therapeutic group home in Atlanta."

Josh in a group home. Away from Jill, the only person in the whole world he cared about. "You can't do that."

But of course, she could.

"We try to keep siblings together, but in this case separating them gives Jill a much better chance of finding a family." Her phone chirped again. "Speaking of, this is the group home coordinator texting now. Just a sec."

Patrick didn't answer, thankful for the chance to collect his thoughts.

He'd known things weren't going well with the kids' parents. They hadn't shown up for their scheduled visits—not one. He'd heard rumors they'd moved out of state and that their substance abuse issues had resurfaced.

He'd been praying they'd turn their lives around. He knew how hard it would be for him when Josh and Jill returned home, but he'd gone into foster care with his eyes wide-open. Healing and reuniting families was the goal, and he'd reminded himself every day that Josh and Jill might only be with him for a short while.

Those reminders hadn't helped. He'd fallen for

the kids the minute he'd laid eyes on them. Jilly, scared out of her wits at being moved abruptly from one home to another—again. Josh, pale with fright himself but blustering and determined to protect his little sister, best he could.

The fear and pain in their eyes had skewered Patrick's heart, but at least they'd had each other to hang on to. If the system split them up...

Mitzi made an irritated noise.

"Something wrong?"

"In this job? Constantly. The group home doesn't have room now. Maybe in a month or two." She chucked her phone back into her bag. "This complicates everything."

Hope stirred in Patrick's heart. "Then let's keep things simple. Don't move the kids. Give me some more time to turn Josh around. Then maybe you can find a family willing to adopt them both."

Mitzi heaved an impatient sigh. "And how exactly do you plan to 'turn Josh around' as you put it? You're not having much success so far."

"Then I'll try something else." Patrick tried to think. "Maybe I could enroll Josh in the sheriff's after-school mentoring program."

"It's at capacity," Mitzi told him. "No space for new kids until they get more funding. And there's already a waiting list."

"Well, then, what about the Hope Center?"

That was a desperate, buy-some-time suggestion. The Hope Center, housed in a donated Victorian home on Oak Street, had provided structured after-school activities for struggling local kids for years. However, at the last foster parent support meeting, he'd heard the place had closed—at least temporarily—after years of sagging attendance, leadership problems and complaints from the neighbors. There'd been hope of a last-ditch save when Ruby Sawyer had taken it over after the last director had quit, but that hadn't worked out. And if Ruby couldn't save the place, nobody could.

Ruby was a local legend among foster parents. The elderly woman had single-handedly raised six hard-to-place foster kids, children who came from tough situations and whose futures looked bleak. She was getting older, though, and managing the center was a demanding job. Two weeks ago, Ruby had collapsed and been rushed to the hospital. Since then, the Hope Center had been closed, and it would probably stay that way. He tried to think of another option while he waited for Mitzi to point that out.

Instead, she looked thoughtful. "The Hope Center," she repeated. "We were discussing that place in our caseworkers' meeting this morning. One of Ruby Sawyer's daughters has agreed to run it until they hire another director. My supervisor told us to encourage our families to take advantage of it."

*Ruby's daughter.* Patrick jolted to attention, his heart thudding. "Which daughter? Ruby has three. Is it Maggie?"

"I don't remember." Mitzi shrugged. "Does it matter?"

It sure did. But he didn't want to explain why to Mitzi, especially not right now. He was already on thin ice as it was.

Anyway, it was probably Maggie. She was married to Neil Hamilton, a local history teacher, and they were foster parents themselves. He couldn't see how she'd find the time to run the center on top of caring for a young family and managing Angelo's, the small eatery she co-owned with her former boss, but that was none of his business.

"I'll talk to Maggie and get Josh signed up for whatever programs she's got planned. I'm sure she can help me get his behavior under control."

Mitzi looked doubtful. "I suppose that might work as a stopgap measure. Mrs. Darnell is a huge supporter of the Hope Center, and she'd be happy to hear one of my placements was getting involved there." She shot him a measuring look. "She also wanted us to ask our parents to volunteer at the center."

Her hint was impossible to miss—and pretty ironic. Mitzi, along with most of Cedar Ridge, didn't trust a Callahan as far as she could throw them. But when somebody needed a car towed or a motor rebuilt—or some free help—they conveniently forgot that.

"I'll help out any way I can." And he would. As long as Josh and Jill could stay together.

Mitzi considered him through narrowed eyes. "All right," she conceded. "If Josh stays out of trouble, and if you get involved at the center, then he and Jill can stay with you while the adoption process moves forward."

"And you'll look for a family that'll adopt both of them."

She shook her head. "Patrick—"

"Separating siblings is a last resort. That was in all the stuff I had to read when I was taking the classes to foster. Has that policy changed?" He paused. "Maybe I should call Mrs. Darnell and ask."

At the mention of her boss, Mitzi blinked. "I'll see what I can do," she hedged.

That didn't sound very encouraging, but before Patrick could argue, there was a rap on the door. Alicia Edwards stuck her head in. "Sorry to interrupt, but I have another meeting scheduled."

"We're done anyway." Mitzi stood. "We've put together a plan, but if Josh causes any more trouble, please call my office immediately."

"I'm sure he won't." The principal gave Patrick an encouraging smile.

He smiled back with more confidence than he

felt, then walked out to collect Josh and Jill, his mind already on the Hope Center.

He hadn't seen the inside of that place since his high school days, but that was about to change. He'd volunteer, he'd fundraise, he'd rebuild the center from the ground up, if that's what it took. The foster care system wasn't splitting up Josh and Jill. He was going to see to it.

He walked into the outer office. Jill had fallen asleep with her head on her brother's chest. Josh had his arms around his sister, his chin resting on top of her head.

He looked defiant—and so sad that a lump formed in Patrick's throat. He needed to get Jill home and give her the next dose of her medicine. Then he'd have another man-to-man talk with Josh about right and wrong, which, going by past experience, wasn't likely to do much good.

First, though, he'd take a short detour and get a closer look at the place he'd just hung all their hopes on.

As Torey Bryant looked around the foyer of the old Victorian home, her sense of what-have-I-gotten-myself-into bloomed into mild panic. Ruby had warned her the place had gone downhill, but this wasn't anything like the Hope Center she remembered.

In her memories, the spacious rooms had been bright and clean and buzzing with productive activity. Now the place echoed emptily, everything was dusty and cluttered, and the bulletin board mounted on the wall still displayed faded Fourth of July decorations.

The Hope Center had fallen apart…and now it was her job to put it back together. She had no idea how she'd pull that off, but she'd have to find a way.

She owed the center and Ruby that much.

As she walked through the musty-smelling rooms, she remembered the first day she'd come here. It had been right after her mom had defied their caseworker, refusing to give up her drug-using, abusive boyfriend so Torey could come back home.

"What does that mean?" Torey had asked the social worker uneasily.

The caseworker hadn't pulled any punches. "That you'll probably stay in foster care until you age out at eighteen."

Torey had sat in the cluttered office, stunned. Her mom—the only blood relative she knew—had officially dumped her. She'd have to stay with Mr. and Mrs. Allbright, an irritable middle-aged couple who fostered kids for the income, for two more years.

It had felt like a prison sentence.

She'd barely listened as the caseworker had prattled on about this wonderful new place in town started by local foster parents. Torey could go there in the afternoons after school until the Allbrights got home from work.

The Hope Center, the caseworker had called it, and Torey had rolled her eyes. So cheesy.

She'd been prepared to hate this place, but to her surprise, it had lived up to its name. She'd found hope here. More accurately, hope, in the form of the center's founder, Ruby Sawyer, had found her.

It hadn't taken Ruby long to see how miserable Torey was, and Ruby never let any kid stay unhappy in her presence if she could help it. She'd pulled strings to get Torey placed in her own home and then she'd tackled the uphill battle of earning Torey's trust.

Torey had learned to trust nobody except herself, but Ruby wasn't the sort who gave up easily. In the end, the scrawny, gray-haired woman had changed Torey's life.

Now it was her turn to help Ruby by nursing her back to health and resurrecting her beloved Hope Center. Ruby's health was coming along fine, but Torey might have bitten off more than she could chew here. Everywhere she looked, something needed fixing.

Like these computers. She ran one finger over the top of a chubby monitor and shuddered, horrified to the bottom of her technology-loving heart. These old clunkers belonged in museums.

Or better yet, dumpsters.

Ruby's voice spoke in her head. *When you got a big job to do, just roll up your sleeves and get started. You don't finish nothing standing still.*

Torey pulled out her phone and started up the wide staircase. She'd begin by making a list of the most obvious problems from the top of the house down to its basement. Then she'd start brainstorming some after-school programs they could offer. She'd be starting from scratch because all the volunteers had quit, fed up with the heavy-handed previous director. Ruby had come out of retirement to try to salvage the place.

That hadn't ended well.

When Torey's foster brother had called to tell her Ruby had been rushed to the hospital, she'd raced out of her Atlanta office, ignoring her new boss's frantic questions. Her heart hadn't beat normally again until she'd made it to Cedar Ridge and seen Ruby for herself, frail but alive and fussing.

"New ain't worn off that job of yours yet," Ruby had whispered. "Gonna get in trouble, missing work so soon."

"I don't care," Torey had whispered back. She hadn't. Her dream job at Gordon Software and her sleek new apartment in midtown hadn't mattered a hill of beans next to Ruby.

Ruby had to be all right. She just had to—and Torey planned to make sure of it. Over Ruby's objections, she'd taken a leave from work and moved home to oversee her foster mom's recovery.

She'd explained the situation to her boss via email, but Cal Gordon had been less than sympathetic. He'd vetoed her request to work remotely—ironic, given the fact that the whole company was geared around software development. He'd given her the three months leave she'd requested, but he'd made it clear he wasn't happy.

She wasn't either. Developing cutting-edge software was a lot easier than nursing Ruby. They'd been butting heads for weeks, especially over the Hope Center. No other director had been found, and when Ruby had threatened to take on the job again, Torey had volunteered to direct the center herself.

Temporarily.

Now she just had to figure out how.

She'd just finished checking the second floor when somebody opened the front door. Frowning, she clicked off the voice recording app she'd been using and moved toward the top of the staircase.

"Sorry, we're clo—" She stopped short, her eyes widening.

A handsome man with short, reddish-brown hair and a clean-shaven, square chin stood on the tile floor of the foyer, flanked by two kids, a boy and a girl. The smudged blue coveralls he wore matched his eyes and strained at his shoulders, which were every bit as broad as she remembered. It couldn't be—but it was.

Patrick Callahan.

Memories dumped over her in a heart-thumping avalanche, like the contents of a neglected closet. Patrick, kicking at stone in the school parking lot as he asked her for a date. And later, laughing at Ruby's kitchen table at countless suppers, playing touch football with her foster brothers and helping them rebuild their patched together cars. Patrick on his knees in a leaky boat on Bluejay Lake, holding up an engagement ring, his eyes—just the color of the lake water—warm and soft as they looked into hers, making promises he wouldn't keep.

A few months later, those same eyes had avoided hers as he'd asked for his ring back. He'd broken her heart that night, and she hadn't felt the same about romance—or her hometown—since.

The hurt ran too deep to be fiddled with, so she'd left it strictly alone. For the past ten years, she'd worked to build a life away from Cedar Ridge, and she'd tried to pretend Patrick Callahan didn't exist.

But of course, he did. And naturally, he'd stroll back into her life, today, looking all blue-collar handsome at a moment when she was feeling grungy and overwhelmed. Wasn't that always the way things worked?

Life was so not fair.

Neither of them spoke. The tension in the room was thick as cream, and the little girl on Patrick's left stirred uneasily. "Who's that lady, Paddy?"

*Paddy.* Torey's heart lurched. She hadn't heard that nickname in years. The Cedar Ridge High School football coach had christened Patrick with that name back when he played on the team, and much to his disgust, it had stuck.

It took Patrick a second to answer. From the look on his face, she wasn't the only one feeling stunned.

A spark of spite flared behind her astonishment. Good.

"That," he said, "is Torey Bryant." Hearing him say her name again gave her an unpleasant quivery feeling, like she felt when she banged her funny bone on a table. He hesitated before adding, "She's one of Mrs. Ruby's daughters. We were…uh. We went to school together."

Well, that stung. They'd been a lot more than classmates. But whatever.

Torey straightened her shoulders. "Hello, Patrick. It's been a minute." She thought about adding that it was nice to see him, but it wasn't, and she'd never been good at telling polite fibs.

"It has." Patrick stared at her, his blue eyes still as startling against his tanned skin as they'd been back in high school. That was the first thing she'd admired about him—his eyes. Then he'd smiled, and that had pushed her heart right over the edge of the cliff.

Ancient history, she reminded herself. She cleared her throat.

"Who've you got with you?" She nodded at the kids.

"Sorry." Patrick glanced down at the boy and girl, and his expression gentled. "This is Josh Pruitt and his sister, Jill."

"Nice to meet you," Torey said. The girl smiled, but the boy stared at her sullenly.

Torey recognized that stare. She'd perfected it when she was a foster kid herself. Most kids who'd spent any time in the child welfare system were wary of adults—particularly overly friendly ones.

When Ruby had mentioned that Patrick had become a foster dad, Torey had stayed silent. She never talked about Patrick, no matter how many times Ruby brought him up. Secretly, though, she'd been impressed. Fostering took an incredible amount of dedication, and heartbreak lurked around every corner. It was hard not to feel warm and fuzzy about a single guy willing to take on a job like that.

Hard. Not impossible.

"Like I was saying," she went on. "The Hope Center's actually closed right now."

"Good." Another male voice spoke up. "The

last thing we need is a bunch of hoodlums running up and down this street again."

Torey was startled. She'd been so distracted by Patrick that she hadn't even noticed Barton Myers standing at the front door.

Just what she needed right now. Barton had recently purchased a home on Radford Street, a few doors down from the Hope Center—and, according to Ruby, had been grousing about the center ever since. In fact, she suspected that the stress of dealing with Myers's constant complaints had been one reason for Ruby's collapse.

"Can I help you, Mr. Myers?" she inquired coldly.

"I saw the vehicles out front. You're not reopening this place, are you?"

"Not right this minute, but that's the plan."

Barton scowled. "We'll see about that. You tell that Ruby woman—"

"Ruby's not well," Torey interrupted. "I'm the only one you'll be talking to. Whatever problems you have with this center, write them down and mail them here. I assure you I'll give them all the consideration they're due."

Her choice of words didn't go unnoticed. "Young lady, I've worked with lawyers often enough to know double-talk when I hear it."

"Good." Torey arched an eyebrow. "I'm glad we understand each other. Close the door on your way out."

He complied with a malicious bang, then stomped down the front steps.

"Nice guy," Patrick remarked dryly.

"Not particularly," she muttered. "No wonder my mom ended up in the hospital."

"I was sorry to hear that Ruby had taken sick. How's she doing?"

His voice gentled when he spoke of Ruby. They'd always gotten along well. Even now, when the rest of her family had no use for Patrick, Ruby still spoke kindly of him.

"Much better," Torey assured him. She hated hearing *Ruby* and *sick* in the same sentence. "Thanks," she added stiffly.

"So, when's the center reopening?"

"I'm not sure. There's a lot to do first. I'll be sure to put a notice in the local newspaper when we're up and running again."

She hoped that would be the end of the discussion, but Patrick stayed where he was, frowning.

Torey sighed and started down the steps. "I'm sorry. Is there something else?"

"Maybe." He seemed to come to a decision. "Jill, Josh, why don't you go out to the backyard for a few minutes?"

Torey started to protest. She wasn't sure it was a good idea for kids to be playing out back unsupervised, although she'd given the yard a once-over when she'd driven up, and the playground equipment seemed solid enough. Before she could object, the kids were gone.

Left alone, she and Patrick studied each other warily. "Have they figured out what caused Ruby's collapse?" he asked.

Torey wasn't sure what to make of this conversation, but since she wanted it over, she answered his question. "They're calling it a cardiac event. Not a heart attack, but too close for comfort." She stopped at the foot of the stairs, keeping a careful distance between them.

"I'd thought she looked worn down at the foster parent meetings." Patrick ran his hand through his hair, the way he did when he was worried. Torey felt irritated that she recognized that. She'd tried to forget everything about this guy, and she'd thought she'd managed it.

Apparently not.

"She'd been working too hard, trying to keep this place running. She should've asked us for help, but she was trying to manage everything herself, like always." Torey glanced around the shabby room. "It was too much for her. The place has really gone downhill since we were kids."

*We.* She shouldn't have said that. If there was one topic she needed to avoid like the plague, it was the fact that once upon a time, she and Patrick had been a *we.*

Thankfully, he didn't seem to notice. "Yeah,

from what I've heard, the center's been strug-gling for a while."

"Looks like it. I've only just taken over, so I'm still figuring everything out." She shook her head. "That's going to take a while because noth-ing's computerized. Which might actually be a blessing, considering that the computers here are almost as old as I am."

Updating the computer systems was the first thing on her agenda. She might not know much about other aspects of running the center, but at least she could handle that. And she liked the idea of the Hope Center kids having upgraded computers.

"Taken over? You're going to be running this place?" The look in Patrick's eyes made her skin prickle. She wasn't sure exactly what it was—dis-belief, disapproval, disappointment? Whatever it was, it definitely started with *dis*.

"I told Ruby I'd serve as interim director, yes."

"Why you and not Maggie?"

Torey lifted an eyebrow. That was a little in-sulting.

"Maggie has her hands full, and I'm the des-ignated "keep Ruby happy" kid at the moment. We've been taking turns. The only thing that's going to keep her happy right now is for this cen-ter to keep plugging along, so that's the plan."

Patrick ran his hand through his hair again. "Are you qualified to run a place like this?"

She frowned. "I'm here, I'm willing, and I have a pulse. Right now, those seem to be pretty much all the qualifications you need. Besides, Ruby wants me to do it, and she never asks anybody for anything."

She didn't know why she was explaining all this. She didn't have to justify herself to Patrick Callahan. She dug her fists down on her hips. "Do we have some kind of problem here? "

"Yeah." He met her gaze without flinching. "I'm afraid we do."

# Chapter Two

Patrick didn't mean to be rude, but this was too important to play around with. He needed to make sure Josh and Jill were adopted together, and if this center was the key to that, he couldn't let anybody mess the place up worse than it already was.

He just wished he was squaring off against somebody other than Torey Bryant.

Anybody, actually.

Thanks to his train wreck of a family, as a teenager Patrick had steered clear of romantic relationships. The last thing he'd needed in his life was more drama. While his cousins were out drinking and chasing girls, he'd spent his weekends holed up in his dad's garage, rebuilding engines.

Then he'd met Torey.

He'd fallen for her hard and fast—and so completely that it still boggled his mind. He'd been seventeen the day he'd accidentally bumped into the sad-eyed, dark-haired girl from his math class in the high school hallway. He'd helped her pick up her scattered books, and as he'd handed them over, he'd offered her an apology and a smile.

She'd smiled back.

He'd never seen her smile before, and suddenly the only thing he'd wanted in the whole world was to make her smile again.

He'd known by the end of their first date that he was in big trouble. She was so quiet and serious that nobody saw it, but Torey Bryant was something special. She wasn't only scary-smart. She was beautiful, too, and that beauty wasn't just skin deep. She had a heart as brave as a lion's.

She was completely out of a Callahan's league.

He knew it. But at the time, it hadn't mattered. She was the only girl for him—it was as simple and as complicated as that.

They'd dated through high school. When the mess with his dad had hit, he'd worried he'd lose her, but Torey had stuck with him without blinking an eye. When she'd turned down a scholarship to Georgia Tech to go to a community college close by, he'd known he should have stopped her. He should have convinced her to go because Torey was way too good for a guy like him. She deserved a better life than he could give her.

Instead, he'd secretly worked for a rival garage

at night so he could buy an engagement ring. He still remembered the look in her eyes when he'd slid it on her finger on the best night of his life.

And the look when he'd asked her to give it back—on the worst one.

That little ring was wrapped up in one of his dad's old handkerchiefs, stuffed in the corner of his dresser drawer. He knew exactly where it was, but he hadn't looked at it since that awful night.

She studied him now, her eyes as sharp as dark glass.

"I don't understand. Are you trying to win an award for grudge-holding? What happened between us—"

"That has nothing to do with this."

She didn't look as if she believed him. "Then what's the problem?"

"Running a center for at-risk kids just seems a little outside of your comfort zone. Don't you have some fancy job in Atlanta now?"

"I just took a job with a software development company, yes."

A computer job. Not surprising. Torey had always loved fiddling with computers, just like Josh. And just like Josh, it had gotten her into trouble.

"A new job? Doesn't sound like it would be so easy to take time off from that." He was fishing— and Torey bit.

"It wasn't. But Ruby needed help, so I'm taking three months of family leave."

Three months. "Oh." He couldn't imagine having a job that allowed you to take off months like that. In his business, when you stopped working, you stopped earning.

Must be nice.

Still, he knew Torey. She was ambitious, and after their breakup she couldn't move to the city quick enough. Coming back to Cedar Ridge even for a short while must have been hard. "That was good of you."

"It's what family does," Torey said shortly. "I didn't plan on spending the time running the Hope Center, but this place means a lot to Ruby, and she was stressing out about it."

He started to tell her that he'd promised Mitzi he'd volunteer here but stopped short. That probably wasn't an option, not with Torey in charge.

Especially not given how his heartbeat stuttered every time she tilted her head in the way he remembered.

That didn't mean anything, of course. It was just an echo of sweetness, like the way you could smell flowers even after somebody had taken them out of a room.

Echo or not, it had his nerves torn up. He wished Torey had stayed down in Atlanta, out of sight and—mostly—out of mind.

An idea occurred to him. It wasn't a great idea,

and he had no idea how he'd make it work, but it was the only thing he could come up with.

"I could do it."

Torey's brow crinkled. "Do what?"

"Run the center until they hire somebody permanent. Then you could get back to your job in Atlanta."

She blinked. "You?" Her eyes narrowed. "Why would you do that?"

He didn't want to go into the details, not when the kids could pop back in at any moment. If Josh had any idea that he might be separated from his sister... There was no telling what the boy might do.

"Josh got in trouble at school today, and his social worker thinks he could benefit from some additional resources. He needs a place like the Hope Center, and I'm sure he's not the only kid who does. I'm no expert either, but I've been through all the foster care training, so I learned a few things about working with struggling kids. And like you said earlier, I'm here, I've got a pulse and I'm willing."

"I don't know," she said slowly. "It's important to Ruby that this place keep going."

"So I'll keep it going."

"Really?" There was that head tilt again. "How?"

He had no idea. "I'll figure it out."

"That won't be easy." She glanced around the

center, and the lines crinkling her forehead deepened. "The Hope Center hasn't exactly kept up with the times. What kid's going to want to come to a place that doesn't even have Wi-Fi? Or decent computers, maybe even some video games?"

"Video games?"

They turned to see Josh walking up the back hall, leading Jill by the hand. He looked at Torey with more interest than Patrick had seen in weeks. "Are you gonna let kids game here?"

"Maybe," Torey said before Patrick could speak. "Would you like that?"

"Are you kidding?" Josh's face lit up. "Yeah! Will you get *Superhero Nation*? And *Warriors of Kadan*?"

"*Superhero Nation*, maybe. *WoK* is a definite no." When Josh groaned, Torey smiled. "Sorry, kiddo. I work at a software company, so you can't sneak a mature rated game past me." She cocked an eyebrow at Patrick. "You're not letting him play *Warriors of Kadan*, are you?"

"I don't think so." Patrick policed what the kid had on his devices, and he limited screen time, but it was an ongoing struggle. Josh was more computer savvy than he was. "You're not playing that game, are you, Josh?"

"You don't let me play nothing, hardly," Josh grumbled.

That was an ongoing complaint. It also wasn't an answer, which meant that Patrick needed to do some digging. A wave of weariness washed over him. Fighting this kid's addiction to screens was exhausting—and confusing. In his opinion, the last thing Josh or any of the other kids needed was more access to computers.

"Josh—" he started, but the kid interrupted him.

"Jill's nose is really gross. Is it time for her medicine?"

Patrick glanced at his watch. "Almost." And the medicine was at the garage. "Hey, Josh? Walk Jilly out to the truck, okay? I'll be right there." He waited until the kids were outside before speaking again. "Let's get this settled. Are you okay with me taking over?"

"That doesn't matter because it's not up to me. Ruby's the head of the board."

"I'll talk to her."

"I'd rather you didn't," Torey said quickly. "I don't want her bothered. But I'll tell her you offered, and we'll see what she thinks."

"Okay. If she has any questions—any questions at all—tell her to give me a call." He felt sure, once she understood the situation, Ruby would be on his side.

Torey didn't look happy, but she nodded. "I'll let you know what she says. If she wants me to step down and let you take over, I will."

"Great."

"As long as you agree to do the same thing if

she wants me to stay on. We're not going to tussle over this and stress her out more. Whatever she says to do, we do it. No questions asked, no arguments. Deal?" She held out her hand.

He hesitated, but he understood her reasoning. He'd just have to pray that Ruby understood his.

When he took her hand, his heart jolted. He hadn't held Torey's hand in a very long time, and at the feel of her slim fingers in his, a thousand memories pounced all at once.

He stood there for a second unable to speak, just holding her hand and staring at her.

"Patrick?" As she spoke his name, Torey gave her hand a tug.

He released it as if it was red-hot. "Sorry," he managed through the sudden thickness in his throat. "Yep. We have a deal. Now I've got to go. The kids are waiting."

"Go ahead. I'll get in touch after I talk to Ruby."

He nodded as he turned away, his cheeks stinging red. He didn't draw an easy breath until he was halfway home, and though he tried his best to answer Jill's prattle, he couldn't remember a word he'd said when he pulled into the driveway.

Which, he told himself, was silly. Whatever he'd felt for Torey years ago was well past its expiration date now, and she'd made it clear she didn't have any soft feelings left for him. For all he knew, she had a boyfriend waiting back in Atlanta.

Which was fine. They'd both gone on and made lives for themselves. Different lives, maybe. But good lives. There was no reason for him to feel so...jarred.

One thing was for sure, though. The sooner Torey left Cedar Ridge, the happier he'd be.

That Friday evening after supper, Torey took a sheet of fresh-from-the-oven cookies out of Ruby's hand and plunked it down on her foster mom's well-scrubbed kitchen table.

"I can handle this," she said for the dozenth time. "Please sit down."

Ruby made a shooing gesture. "Stop fussing. I'm fine."

Despite Torey's jumpy nerves, the familiar protest lifted her heart. Ruby had perked up amazingly, and her hazel eyes were sparkling with their usual lively interest.

Maybe Torey wasn't looking forward to tonight's meeting with Patrick, but Ruby clearly was.

When she'd mentioned Patrick's offer, she'd expected Ruby to make a decision then and there. Instead, her foster mom had gone silent for several seconds, her brow wrinkled in thought.

Then she'd called Patrick and invited him over to "talk things out."

"You don't mind, do you?" she'd asked afterward, shooting Torey a sharp look.

"Why should I mind?"

She didn't mind—exactly. It was just that, since this was the first time Patrick had visited the farmhouse since their breakup, tonight might feel a little…awkward.

Bumping into him at the Hope Center certainly had. Torey wasn't a fan of awkward. Or, for that matter, of Patrick.

On the other hand, if seeing him made Ruby feel this much better, it was worth a few cringes.

Torey slid the second sheet of chocolate-pecan cookies into the oven, as Ruby picked up a spatula and began transferring hot cookies to a waiting plate.

"Why'd Maggie send so much cookie dough?" Her foster sister's cookies were legendary, but this seemed like too much of a good thing.

"Your sister's never stingy when it comes to cookies. That's all right. I'll send the extras home with Patrick for the kids to eat." Ruby sighed. "I sure hated to hear Mitzi took over as his caseworker after Jane Anderson retired. That woman tries my patience." Ruby set the empty baking sheet on the stovetop to cool.

Since Ruby's patience was as legendary as Maggie's cookies, that didn't reflect well on Mitzi. Still, Torey couldn't resist adding, "In all fairness, Patrick might not be the easiest guy to work with."

"He's got a stubborn streak, all right. Just like somebody else I could mention." Ruby gave Torey a measuring look. "Whatever somebody tells you to do, you're bound and determined to do the opposite. And Mitzi ain't got enough sense to know that the more you push a stubborn person the more they pull in the opposite direction."

Before Torey could think up a good answer, a twinkle of light caught her eye. She glanced out the window, and her heart thumped. Headlights were coming up the mountain towards Ruby's farmhouse.

"He's here," she said gloomily. "This should be fun."

She switched on the coffeemaker and turned to find Ruby studying her.

"Best not to let past hurts clutter up your heart, honey. They take up too much room. Best to clean 'em out and forget about 'em. Or better yet, patch 'em up and turn 'em back into the joys they were always meant to be."

Torey shot Ruby a suspicious glance. "What's that supposed to mean?" Her foster mom had recently developed a habit of matchmaking. She'd successfully nudged matches for Torey's sister Maggie and her brothers Logan and Ryder. Torey had an awful suspicion that she was next on Ruby's to-do list.

"Only that if you and Patrick was to take a good

look at each other now—a real good look—you might be surprised at how well you get along."

"Oh, no you don't!" Torey protested, alarmed. "Ruby, don't you dare start trying to pair me up with Patrick Callahan. I am not interested. Seriously. Not. Interested."

"Don't get prickly." Ruby patted her arm. "'Course you ain't interested in Patrick. You got that nice job now and a bright future all lined up, and he's sunk his roots so deep here couldn't nothing nor nobody move him. But that don't mean you two shouldn't forgive each other and be friends. Now I'm going to go on in the living room and sit down. I'll take these cookies along, and you can bring the coffee when it's ready."

"I'll pull these other cookies out, too. The timer hasn't gone off, but I'm sure they're close enough."

"No, best give them their full time. If you rush 'em, they'll fall to pieces." The older woman smirked. "They're a lot like people thataway."

What was that supposed to mean? Torey threw her mom another suspicious look, but there was no time to argue. A car door slammed. "Fine. I'll wait on the cookies. You go let Patrick in."

Her plan to hide out in the kitchen backfired. A minute later she heard Ruby saying, "Let's take these back to the kitchen, Patrick."

The door opened, and Ruby walked in, followed by Patrick, who carried a pot of golden chrysanthemums.

"Look at what Patrick brought," Ruby said.

"You always had mums on the table during the fall." Patrick glanced briefly at Torey, then looked back at Ruby.

True. Torey had forgotten that. She should've bought Ruby mums herself.

"Fancy your remembering after all these years. Thank you kindly, Patrick."

"You're welcome," he said, giving Ruby a warm side hug.

Torey's heart panged hollowly. It felt… strange…seeing Patrick here again, hugging Ruby, acting like he still belonged.

Once he had belonged in this kitchen. He'd been welcomed here—after a good going over by her brothers—because Torey liked him. In time, they'd grown to like Patrick for himself, and the night Torey had come home with his diamond glinting on her finger, everyone had cheered. They'd loved the idea of Patrick becoming an official family member.

The memory made Torey flinch. She opened the oven, and a hot, cookie-scented puff of air warmed her cheeks.

"Good. These are almost done," she murmured. "I'm sure Patrick needs to get home to the kids soon, so we'd better get started."

"That's true," Patrick agreed quickly. "I left

them with another foster family, but I'd like to get back early."

"Patrick, why don't you have a seat in the living room?" Torey was anxious to get him in a more neutral location. "We'll be right there."

"Never mind that." Ruby rummaged in a cupboard, emerging triumphantly with pottery pumpkin salt and pepper shakers that her foster son Nick had bought in an open-air market in Mexico City. She set them on either side of the mums and smiled. "Patrick's never been living room company, and besides, I want to enjoy my flowers. Patrick, run grab that plate of cookies off the coffee table. Then we'll talk this Hope Center business out."

Soon they'd settled around the kitchen table, cookies and steaming mugs in front of them. Torey normally drank her coffee black, but she added cream and stirred it just to have something to do with her hands.

She wasn't usually this fidgety, but at least she wasn't the only one. Patrick kept tapping the side of his mug with one finger, and he was very careful not to look in Torey's direction.

His nerves hadn't affected his appetite, though. He was already on his third cookie.

"So." Ruby fortified herself with a sip of coffee before forging ahead. "It's a real blessing both of you are willing to step in and run the center while we look for a permanent replacement. Always better to have more than you need than not enough, but it sure makes for a hard decision. Maybe I better hear what you each think needs doing to turn the Hope Center around. Patrick, since you're our guest, you go first."

Patrick rubbed his jaw. "I've been thinking about that. The building's sound. It just needs a good cleaning and a few minor repairs that I could take care of myself. As for what the Hope Center does, I think help with homework is important, and there should be some focus on encouraging good behavior at home and at school. Some kids struggle with that."

"Like your Josh." Ruby had never been one to beat around the bush.

"That's right, but he's not the only one. I reached out to a couple of local youth pastors, and they said they'd love to help out with that part."

"Good idea," Ruby said. "Anything else?"

"I believe we should set up classes to teach the kids life skills."

Ruby paused, her coffee cup at her lips. "Like what?"

"Things like basic auto repair. I could teach that myself. Maybe some simple home maintenance. Budgeting, childcare, how to dress and act at a job interview, all the stuff that most kids learn from their moms and dads."

Torey shifted in her seat.

"What is it, Torey?" When she didn't immediately answer, Ruby added, "You got something to say, you say it. That's what this meeting's for. What Patrick said makes sense to me. If you got different ideas, I'd like to hear them."

Torey glanced at Patrick. He returned her gaze steadily, as if daring her to speak her mind.

Fine. She would.

"Those are good ideas, but you won't draw today's kids there by promising to teach them how to fix the kitchen sink. Attendance is way down. I know you'd hate to see the place close, Ruby, but what's the point of keeping it open if hardly any kids are coming? We should start by making the center an interesting place to be."

A few ticks of thoughtful silence followed her pronouncement. Then Ruby asked, "And how do you propose to do that?"

"For starters, by making some updates. The Hope Center is a relic, and today's kids eat, sleep, and breathe technology. They aren't going to flock to a place with no Wi-Fi and ancient computers."

Ruby furrowed her brow. "I don't think you're wrong about that. Patrick? What do you say?"

"Maybe Torey's right about making the place more interesting, but if you ask me, the last thing kids need is another place to play video games."

Torey frowned. "I'm not saying the kids should spend all their time playing games, but computer literacy is an important skill. Since most of these kids don't have access to top-of-the-line devices at home, they're already behind. And," she went on, "whether we like it or not, kids are attracted to screens, so having access to quality devices will be a big draw."

"But how will we pay for those quality devices?" Ruby asked. "The Hope Center's budget is pretty skimpy."

"I can finagle some donations," Torey said. "People in my business update their equipment religiously, and their castoffs would be worlds better than what the kids have now." Worlds better that what most of the citizens of Cedar Ridge had in their own homes, too, but she didn't mention that.

"Well." Ruby studied her half-empty coffee cup. "Both of you have made some good points."

A tickle crawled up Torey's spine. She recognized the expression on her foster mom's face.

Ruby was up to something.

Patrick cleared his throat. "They're really different points, though. It boils down to which way you want to go."

"That's just the trouble. I want to go both ways. And the truth is," she went on, "I don't see no reason to pick. You two can just run the Hope Center together."

Torey sucked in a startled breath and shot a glance at Patrick. He'd jerked bolt upright in his chair and looked as alarmed as she felt.

"I don't think—" Torey protested, but Ruby cut her off.

"You've already said you was each willing to do the job," the older woman pointed out. "It'll be easier with a partner to help out, won't it? Between the two of you, we'll have all the computer stuff brought up to date, and lots of old-fashioned activities lined up for the kids, too." She leaned back in her chair, looking pleased. "As long as you two cooperate with each other, things should balance out real nice."

Torey stole another glance at Patrick and found him staring back at her, looking as if somebody had knocked the wind out of him.

"That's settled then!" Ruby announced before either of them could speak. "Now, I'm a little tired, but you don't mind clearing up the kitchen, do you, Torey?"

"No, of course not." Torey studied her mom suspiciously. Ruby didn't seem tired. She looked perkier than she had in weeks.

"I'm sure Patrick'll pitch in."

Ah, there it was. "You don't have to—"

Patrick interrupted her. "I'm happy to help."

Ruby gave him an approving pat on the shoulder as she rose from her seat. "You can talk about how you're going to get the Hope Center back on track. I can't wait to see what you come up with."

She disappeared down the hall toward her bedroom, a new spring in her step. Avoiding Patrick's eyes, Torey gathered their cups and saucers and retreated to the sink. As she ran hot soapy water in the old enamel basin, her relief battled with annoyance.

Ruby was improving by leaps and bounds, and that was wonderful. They'd all been so worried about her.

On the other hand, she was obviously up to her old tricks. Torey hoped Patrick hadn't caught on that Ruby was trying to nudge them together. This was ridiculous—and embarrassing. She'd have to have a talk with Ruby and make it clear that—

"That was unexpected." Patrick spoke right behind her, and the cup she was washing slipped into the dishwater with a splash.

"It sure was. I want you to know I had absolutely nothing to do with it."

"Nope, you made it pretty clear that you don't like my ideas."

He was talking about them codirecting the Hope Center, not Ruby's heavy-handed matchmaking. Torey felt a flush of relief. This she could deal with.

"You don't like mine, either."

"I guess that's true." Patrick turned to retrieve the plate of cookies. As he reached past her to set it on the scarred counter, Torey caught a scent straight out of her memories. The metallic smell of an engine mixed with laundry detergent and a hint of orange. Her heart hammered, and her gaze dropped to his hands.

Sure enough, his fingers were red. He'd scrubbed them before coming over. Patrick worked elbow deep in oil and grease, and his hands were blackened by the end of the day. Back in high school, he'd been self-conscious about that. He'd always scoured his hands with an orange-scented hand soap before taking her on a date, scrubbing so savagely that he usually removed some skin along with the grease.

Concerned, she'd told him to quit worrying about it. She didn't care if there were smudges on his hands.

*I care.* She still remembered the fierceness in his voice. *I never want you to have cause to be ashamed of me, Torey. Never.*

"I had a lot of good times in this kitchen," he murmured now, as if he was talking to himself. "Funny. Even after all these years, it looks just the same."

He sounded so wistful that Torey's heart softened, but she didn't know what to say. Maybe Ruby's kitchen hadn't changed since the old days, but everything else sure had.

They had.

Maybe Patrick was thinking the same thing, because he sighed. "I know Ruby means well, Torey, but I'm not sure how we're going to make this partner thing work."

"I have no idea, either," she said. "I can try to talk her out of it, but you know Ruby. She complains about other people being stubborn, but she's the world's worst. Once she's made up her mind, she won't budge."

"We'll have to figure it out, then." He fished in his pocket, producing a business card with *Callahan's Motors* written in green script next to the silhouette of an antique roadster. "Give me a call tomorrow, and we'll work out a time to get together and make some plans."

Torey accepted the card, careful to make sure their fingers didn't touch. "All right."

The silence stretched out just a second too long, and Patrick cleared his throat. "I'd better get going. I need to pick up the kids."

"That's fine. You know the way out," she said, keeping her eyes on the dishes she was washing. She lingered in the kitchen until she heard Patrick start up his truck.

Then she went in search of Ruby. She found her sitting in her bedroom armchair, looking bright-eyed and not the least bit tired.

"Ruby Sawyer," Torey said sternly. "This may be the most ridiculous stunt you've ever pulled. Just so there's no misunderstanding, I'm going to say it straight out. Patrick Callahan and I aren't getting back together, no matter what you do."

Her foster mother looked unperturbed. "Never said you ought to. Sometimes it's best to let sleeping dogs lie. I'm just asking you two to cooperate with each other for the good of the Hope Center. Surely you can manage that."

"And if we can't?"

Ruby shrugged. "The way I see it, this'll go one of two ways. Either you two will be the saving of that center, or you'll pull the poor place down around your ears." She chuckled, a sassy glint in her eye that Torey hadn't seen in a long while. "Either way, it's gonna be real interesting to watch."

# Chapter Three

The following Monday afternoon, Patrick was in his garage, beaming his flashlight into the engine of a 1954 Ford Customline. Jill stood on a wooden step stool beside him, peering under the hood with interest.

He sneaked a glance at his watch. In about an hour, he and Torey were sitting down together to make decisions about the center, and he was getting nervous.

He'd burned some midnight oil looking for interesting ways to rekindle the center. He thought he'd come up with a winner, but he wasn't sure Torey would go for it.

"Ask me another one!" Jill demanded, breaking into his thoughts. She'd felt well enough to rejoin her kindergarten class today. Josh, who was still sitting out his suspension, had spent the day glumly doing his school assignments in Patrick's office.

By the time Jill had scampered off the school bus at the garage, there hadn't been enough time to go home before his meeting, so he was passing the time showing Jill the various parts of the vintage engine. He figured it was good practice in case he ended up teaching an auto repair class at the center.

He'd offered to teach Josh, too, but that idea had gone nowhere.

"All right, Jillybean, let's go for the gold." He focused the flashlight. "What's that?"

"Radiator," she announced. "That's too easy, Paddy!"

*Paddy.* Every time she called him that, it made him grin. He'd gone with his old nickname because it sounded nonthreatening. Sort of friendly and a little bit goofy. Recently another idea had occurred to him.

It wasn't a far jump to *Daddy.*

He'd been thinking about that a lot since Mitzi had mentioned Josh and Jill would be available for adoption. Usually, the current foster parents were given the first opportunity to adopt children in their care. He doubted that would apply to him, given Mitzi's attitude and Josh's behavioral problems. But after a lot of pondering and praying, he'd figured there was no harm in asking.

However, before he brought the subject up with Mitzi, he needed to get things straightened out with Josh. He glanced at the boy. He was slumped on a bench against the wall of the garage, looking bored.

*Keep trying.* Patrick cleared his throat. "Sure you don't want to take a turn, Josh?"

"Nah." Josh breathed out the word on a weary sigh. "I don't know nothing about engines."

His tone made it clear that he didn't want to know anything about them, either. Patrick smothered a sigh of his own. When he'd been Josh's age, he'd loved spending time in his dad's garage. At least until he'd discovered half Ron Callahan's income came from parting out luxury cars his nephews stole. RC's Hometown Garage was a cover for a high-end chop shop.

Even all these years later, the memory made Patrick sick. It wasn't just that his father had turned out to be just like the rest of the Callahans, although that was bad enough. Ron had always insisted that he and Patrick were different. *The two goody-goodies of a baddy-bad family, that's us,* Ron had joked.

That had been a lie. His dad must've been on the wrong side of the law for at least a decade before Patrick found out. And all that time, he'd been unwittingly helping his father and his cousins rip people off.

Water under the bridge, he reminded himself. He'd done what he could to set things right, and that's all he could do.

"Come on, guys." He set Jill carefully on the

ground. "It's about time for my meeting with Miss Torey at the Hope Center."

Josh's face brightened. "Maybe she's got the internet hooked up!"

Patrick kept his face carefully neutral. "Maybe. But you're on screen restriction until your suspension's up, remember?"

Josh groaned, but a look from Patrick sent him back into his silent sulk.

"Don't be mad, Joshie," Jill pleaded. "We can still play in the backyard. That's fun, too."

"Fun for you, maybe," her brother muttered. But when his sister's face fell, he reached over and tugged on her ponytail. Then he made a goofy face, sending her into a fit of giggles.

Patrick set his jaw. Josh had problems, but the kid loved his little sister with all his heart. That would be the key to reaching him. But if he was separated from her...

Not going to happen, Patrick promised himself grimly.

Josh didn't speak another word until they pulled up at the Hope Center. Then he straightened in his seat, his eyes wide.

"Wow!"

Two vans, emblazoned with the logo of the local internet provider, were parked in front of the Victorian home. A truck with Johnson's Electrical printed on its door blocked the driveway.

They found Torey deep in an animated discussion with a guy from the internet service while two other men crouched in front of a phone jack in the front room, fiddling with wires. Sounds of drills and hammering came from other regions of the house.

"Hey," Patrick shouted above the din. "What's going on?"

She blinked. "Patrick! Is it time for our meeting already?" She looked at her watch and grimaced. "It is. Stan, give me a minute, okay?"

Leaving the uniformed guy, she walked in his direction. Today she wore faded blue jeans, and a gray T-shirt that hugged her slim frame. Her dark hair was pulled back into a ponytail that poked out of the back of a ball cap, and her eyes sparkled with enthusiasm.

Patrick's stomach flipped upside down. All she needed was a stack of books in her arms, and she could've walked right out of his high school memories—the best ones, the ones so sweet that he never let himself think about them.

She flashed a smile at Jill and Josh. "Hiya. You feeling better, kiddo?"

Jill nodded. "Lots."

"Good."

"Is the Wi-Fi hooked up?" Josh interjected hopefully.

"Josh—" Patrick started wearily.

"I'm just *asking*."

Torey chuckled. "These guys are working on

it. And guess what's in those boxes?" She nodded toward a row of cardboard packages against the foyer wall.

Patrick's gut tightened. Uh-oh.

"New computers?" Josh's voice squeaked with excitement.

"Newer." Torey winked. "Which isn't saying much, considering what was here before. But trust me, these will be a huge improvement."

"Can I look at them?"

"Josh—" Patrick interjected again.

"No, it's all right," Torey assured him. She grinned at the boy. "Just be careful, okay?"

"I will!" Josh didn't wait for a second invitation. He raced to open the flaps of a carton. His exclamation of awe and delight made Torey laugh and sparked Jill's curiosity. The little girl turned loose of Patrick's hand and trotted over to join her brother.

"I wanna see, Joshie!"

Torey's eyes lingered on the children, the softness in their dark depths doing more funny things to the pit of Patrick's stomach.

He pushed the feelings aside. "What's going on?" He gestured toward the men.

Torey was watching Josh oohing and aahing over the computer. She looked back at him, her eyebrows going up.

"They're getting the internet connected. It was

more involved than I expected. The building's electrical system needed some tweaking."

"You arranged this without running it by me?"

She frowned, looking confused. "I was going to tell you about it at our meeting today. It was no easy feat to get these guys in here so fast. They were clear if I wanted the job done in the time frame I mentioned, they'd need to get started right away."

Patrick stood silent for a minute, keeping a hold on his temper. Then he said, "This seems like something we should have talked about ahead of time."

"It was last minute, and like I said, there wasn't any flexibility in their schedules." Torey spoke absently, her eyes already drifting back to the electricians and technicians.

"Look," Patrick said, sharply enough that her attention refocused on him. "I'm no happier about this arrangement than you are, but when it comes to running the center, you and I are equals. Things like this—" he gestured at the men, "—should be cleared with me."

Torey's eyes widened, then narrowed. "*Cleared* with you? I'm the one in charge of updating the tech."

"You may be the expert on that, and it may be your responsibility, but you're not the only one in charge," Patrick pointed out. "This could've waited until we'd talked it over."

"No," Torey retorted, her voice cool and sharp. "It couldn't. These guys are the best, and they're booked solid. They're doing me a favor, so I had to work with their schedules."

"A favor?" Patrick didn't like the sound of that. "Be careful, Torey. There can't be anything shady going on here."

"Shady?" A flash of temper sparked into Torey's eyes. "For pity's sake, Patrick, I just offered to help the electricians set up a better web page in exchange for quick work and a discount. And a friend of mine works in management for the company providing the internet here, and he owed me a favor."

"All that needs to be written down, and any outside-the-box arrangements you make ought to be cleared with the board. And with me." After his father's arrest, he'd battled too many side glances and whispers. He'd worked hard to rebuild his reputation, and he couldn't risk losing it. Especially not right now, not with Mitzi watching him like a hawk and Josh's and Jill's futures hanging in the balance.

Torey made an impatient noise. "I explained already that this couldn't wait. These guys—"

He shook his head. "No shortcuts, Torey. Not while you're working with me. I know how badly you want to save this center for Ruby's sake, but—"

"I'm not doing anything wrong here, Patrick!"

She studied him, a pulse fluttering angrily in her neck. "I don't see why you can't understand that."

"Maybe because I've heard that line before."

Disbelief flashed in her eyes, followed by a chill he felt all the way to his bones. "Oh, I see." Her chest rose with quick, uneven breaths. "I wondered how long it would be before you dredged that up."

For a second he wasn't sure what she meant. He'd been talking about his dad, who'd assured him for years that he wasn't doing anything wrong.

Then he caught on, and his heart thudded to a stop. He tried to think of something to say, but there wasn't anything that would help. Not now.

He'd just stepped on a land mine and there was nothing to do but wait for the explosion.

"You broke up with me over it," she pointed out icily. "Wasn't that enough?"

He didn't answer. That wasn't why he'd broken their engagement, but it had made a good excuse—the only one she'd have accepted.

When he remained silent, Torey made an exasperated noise. "At least be fair. I never lied to you about what I did."

He should probably stay silent, but she was splitting hairs. "You didn't tell me about it, either." Not until the police had come knocking on his door with a warrant.

Her cheeks went ruddy. "I had no idea it would cause such a big problem."

"You hacked into a national testing service website and changed a test score, Torey. Of course, it was going to cause a problem."

"Two points. I changed your score by two points so you could get the scholarship at the tech school for that automotive certification you needed. And yes, it was a stupid, wrong thing to do, and I'm sorry I did it. But that was a long time ago, and it has nothing to do with me trading some professional favors for a speedy internet installation."

She had a point, and it was high time they dropped this hot potato subject anyway. "I'm sorry." He nodded toward Josh and Jill. "It's just that I have a lot to lose, so I can't afford to take any risks."

"Well, you can relax." She lifted her chin. "For one thing, I'm not a lovestruck twenty-year-old anymore. And believe it or not, my judgment's improved over the last ten years. Apparently," she muttered, "that makes one of us."

Patrick flinched. He recognized the tone in her voice—hurt mingled with embarrassment and indignation. She'd sounded just the same way that night, that terrible night when he'd made the decision to let her go.

To make her go. For her own good. And for his.

His heart pounded and his mouth went dry. He needed to get out of here. Now.

"Josh, Jill, come on. We're leaving."

"What about our meeting?" Torey called after him impatiently. "Obviously we have things we need to talk about."

"We've said enough for now." He spoke without turning around, shepherding the two protesting kids out the front door. He was almost home before his heart slowed down, and as he pulled into his driveway; he faced the truth head-on. This wasn't going to work out. There was just no way he could spend time with Torey and keep his head on straight.

No stinking way.

Three hours later, Torey drove her Mustang past the city limits sign, heading toward Patrick's house. Her palms were so sweaty they slid on the steering wheel, so she wiped them one by one on her jeans.

She shouldn't be nervous. It was an apology, that's all. She'd messed up.

It had taken her two hours to realize that, and another half hour to decide to apologize.

She'd been too focused on getting the center's new internet system up and running, and she'd bulldozed ahead. She was so used to working alone that it hadn't occurred to her to ask for Patrick's input.

She didn't blame Patrick for being annoyed with her for not checking with him. She should have simply apologized and promised to do better in the future. Instead, they'd gotten into an argument and raked up bad memories.

They both had been ignoring the past, even as it hovered around them like a bad smell. Today they'd broken that unspoken truce by dragging old hurts up front and center.

Maybe that was a good thing. Maybe this would clear the air, so they could work together without all the tension.

And who knew? Maybe by spending time with Patrick, she'd put that old heartbreak behind her once and for all. It had hurt when Patrick had turned his back on her. She knew she'd done the wrong thing, changing that score, but she'd admitted it, apologized and cut a deal involving a long stint of community service to make amends.

She'd expected Patrick to forgive her, to understand she'd made the mistake with the best of intentions—because she loved him. She'd expected him to forgive her—because she thought he'd loved her back.

Instead, he'd broken up with her, and she'd never gotten over that. It was high time she did. Ruby always said forgiveness was a balm to the soul, and for years her soul had felt like it had a bad case of nettle rash.

It was worth a try. Avoiding him like the plague sure hadn't helped.

Torey pulled her Mustang into Patrick's driveway and parked. She hesitated, considered the small bakery box resting on the passenger seat.

Should she or shouldn't she?

She set her mouth in a determined line and picked up the box. She owed him an olive branch. Maybe this would show him that she remembered the good as well as the bad—and maybe it would help him do the same.

As she got out of her car, she eyed Patrick's house with interest. She'd seen the place before, of course. In fact, she'd suspended the whole Patrick-doesn't-exist thing a couple of times and gone out of her way to pass by here, driven by a secret curiosity. She'd wanted to see what sort of home her ex had built for himself.

A pretty one.

The modest two-story was painted yellow, with crisp white trim and a bright blue door. It boasted a wide, welcoming front porch, complete with a swing. It was located outside of town, surrounded by small fields, the sheltering mountains towering overhead. A fence, an actual white picket fence, enclosed a neat yard. In spring and early summer, the fence was festooned with climbing roses, but the vines were cut back now, ready for fall.

It was a storybook house; the house Patrick had described when they'd daydreamed together about their future all those years ago. He'd built it without her.

She walked up a pebbled path, past a hay bale

where a life-sized smiling scarecrow sat with two smaller ones, a boy and a girl. The big one wore coveralls and a ball cap with Callahan's Motors in script on the front. The girl had straw pigtails.

Lopsided ones.

Torey's heart twinged. Trust Patrick to have not just one scarecrow for decoration, but a whole family. His voice echoed in her memory. *Let's have lots of kids, Torey. I'm willing to work hard, but I don't want fancy trips or a new truck or anything like that. If I have you and a houseful of kids, then I'll be happy for the rest of my life.*

At the time, she'd wanted that too, more than anything. Now the memory dug at her like a splinter.

She knocked on a door festooned with a shock of multicolored corn. A few seconds later, Patrick opened it, dressed in jeans and a white T-shirt, with feet covered in socks and his reddish-brown hair disheveled. He looked at her, his brows drawn together.

"Torey?" *What are you doing here?*

He didn't ask the question, but she read it in his eyes. She swallowed hard.

"I wondered—could we talk for a minute?" She wiggled the bakery box. "I brought a peace offering."

"Sure." He opened the door wider. "Come in."

She stepped into a comfortably cluttered family room. The sofa, armchairs and carpet were all stylishly neutral and matched a little too well, making her suspect that Patrick had ordered a complete room setup from some furniture showcase. But there were splashes of his personality here and there, too.

A collection of model cars was displayed on built-in bookshelves beside stacks of parts catalogs and reference books. Antique metal signs advertising oil and other garage supplies hung on the cream-colored walls. A wooden desk stood in the far corner, holding a battered laptop. Papers were mounded beside it, a wrench serving as a paperweight. A jacket was tossed over the back of the office chair, and toys were scattered over the floor. Two school book bags were on the coffee table, and the room smelled of motor oil and crayons.

And oranges. Torey's heart thumped.

"Have a seat," Patrick invited. Torey perched on the edge of the sofa as Patrick settled into a large leather chair.

"So," she said. "I'll start by saying I'm sorry about what happened today."

"So am I. I've had a lot on my mind, and I overreacted."

Okay. So far so good. She handed him the box. "I hope you still like these."

Patrick lifted the lid. His face didn't change expression as he looked at its contents. "Chocolate cupcakes."

"Three so you can share with Josh and Jill."

Patrick studied her, something she couldn't quite identify glimmering in his eyes. Surprise, maybe? Regret? She couldn't tell.

He leaned back in the recliner. "Thanks."

She waited, but he didn't say anything else. She was a little surprised—and disappointed. She'd counted on the cupcakes to be an icebreaker.

A month after they'd started dating, Patrick's birthday had rolled around. He hadn't said a word, and when she'd realized the day had passed without any sort of celebration, she'd fussed at him. Patrick had seemed genuinely bewildered. He and his dad had never paid much attention to birthdays, so he'd not seen the point of mentioning it.

*No birthday cake? Nothing?* she'd asked him. *Not since I was four, when my mom left. I don't care. Birthdays are for little kids, anyhow.*

Thanks to her negligent mom, Torey had missed too many birthdays of her own to believe him. The next day she'd stashed a cupcake in his locker. Nothing special, just a chocolate cupcake in a brown paper sack with Happy Birthday scribbled on it. Then every Tuesday for the next several weeks she'd done the same thing until he'd had one for every birthday he'd missed, plus an extra "to grow on" as Ruby put it.

After that, cupcakes had become their thing. When one of them needed to apologize to the other, a cupcake appeared in a locker or on the

seat of a car. When there was something to celebrate, cupcakes. That Christmas, Patrick had
given her a silver necklace with a cupcake charm
dangling from it.

Fine. If he wouldn't bring up the elephant in
the room, she would.

"This—you and me thing—it's awkward,
given the history we have," she said bluntly. "I
know we were both trying to ignore that, but obviously it's not working. I think it might help if
we're just—" she shrugged "—up-front about
everything."

He was silent for a second. Then he nodded.
"Fine. You go first."

Fair enough. "We need to leave the past in the
past. Agreed?"

"Do you think we can?"

"I can." Torey said firmly.

He considered her for a long second. "Okay.
Then I guess I can, too."

"Good. Second, I shouldn't have set up the internet installation without talking with you about
it. I'm sorry. I wasn't trying to leave you out of
the loop. Since technology is my area of expertise, I felt confident going ahead."

"Maybe you know more about computers, but
I might have a better grasp of what the kids in
Cedar Ridge need. And," he added pointedly,
"what they don't need."

"What's that supposed to mean?"

"Look…" Patrick ran a hand through his hair, ruffling it up even more. "I've only been a parent for a few months, but I can tell you that managing screen time is one of my biggest headaches. Josh and I have tangled over that more than once, and when he gets in trouble at school there's always a computer involved. He needs fewer screens and more face-to-face time with adults and other kids, and I'm sure he's not the only one."

Torey tried to think of the best way to navigate this diplomatically.

"I understand your concern, but the Hope Center has to adapt to stay relevant to kids. That means having quality computers and internet access."

He looked unconvinced, but he shrugged. "Well, it's already done, so I guess that's a moot point. But screen time should be balanced with other activities. And from now on, we make all decisions together."

"What about when we can't agree?" Which, she estimated, would be about 90 percent of the time.

From the look on Patrick's face, he knew that, too. "How about we let Ruby be the tiebreaker? Unless you think it would stress her out too much."

Torey considered. "I think she'd like being involved." Maybe a little too much. "I'll ask her about it." She stood and hesitated, as something occurred to her. "Although…getting Ruby in the middle of this might cause a different problem."

"What kind of problem?"

Torey didn't want to mention this—she really didn't. But she'd probably better. Ruby had all the subtlety of a wrecking ball. "She's got this nutty idea in her head. She's determined to see all of us kids matched up and settled down, and I'm next in line."

"That so?" Patrick rose and started toward the door. "She got somebody in mind for you?"

He still wasn't getting it. Torey sucked in a steadying breath. "Yeah. You."

He turned, his face blank with astonishment. *"What?"*

"I think it's ridiculous, too," Torey said defensively. "And I'm worried she might pull some stunt to try to push us together."

Patrick appeared to think that over. "Maybe she already has. She's got us working together at the Hope Center. You think that's part of a matchmaking scheme?"

"I wouldn't rule it out. And knowing Ruby, she'll keep at it, so I want you to know that— whatever happens, it's not my idea." She tried a joke. "I didn't want you to think I was throwing myself at you or anything."

Patrick's lips twitched. Then he started laughing.

And he kept laughing.

She narrowed her eyes. It wasn't *that* funny.

"Throwing yourself at me." He guffawed one last time and wiped his eyes. "Maybe I'm not as book smart as you are, Torey, but trust me. That's something I could've figured out on my own, no matter what kind of stunt Ruby pulled. Although you might want to skip bringing me cupcakes next time, just to stay on the safe side." He laughed again and shook his head as he reached for the doorknob. "I'll see you at the center on Monday. We'll talk more then."

He was still chuckling when he closed the door behind her.

# Chapter Four

The bolt Patrick was tightening on the exhaust manifold snapped, jerking his attention back to the car he was working on. He viewed the damage with disgust.

It was the second time that had happened today. He never overtightened bolts, but he'd been making careless mistakes all morning. It was annoying—and oddly familiar.

The last time he'd had this much trouble keeping his mind on his work had been back when he and Torey were dating. Now she was back in his life—sort of—and here he was, zoning out again.

He had to snap out of this.

The phone rang. Grateful for the interruption, he stepped out from under the car lift and tucked the ratchet in his pocket.

"Callahan's Motors," he said, cradling the phone between his cheek and his shoulder as he wiped his fingers with a grease rag.

"You got time to trade a few words with an old lady? Fair warning. I'm calling to ask for a favor."

Patrick froze in midwipe as he recognized the voice. Ruby.

He took a second before he responded. "I'm happy to help you out any way I can. You having car trouble?"

"Can't have car trouble if you ain't driving." She sounded irritated. "Doctor won't clear me for that until my next checkup. No, I'm calling about something else. Torey told me you two are having a meeting this afternoon at the Hope Center."

"That's right." It would be the first time they'd seen each other in person since she'd come to his house.

With cupcakes.

That gesture had taken him by surprise, and he still hadn't completely recovered. He'd given the kids' theirs, but he'd stuck his in the pantry, unsure what to do with it.

The truth was, he hadn't eaten a cupcake in over ten years. Cupcakes brought up memories of Torey—always. And he'd needed to keep those memories locked up good and tight.

"That's what I called about," Ruby was saying now. "I never like going behind my young 'uns' backs, but in this case, I'm making an exception. I need you to do something for me, and I'm gonna have to ask you to keep it to yourself."

Patrick frowned, recalling the last thing Torey

had mentioned—that Ruby had some off-the-wall idea about pairing them up. That had been an even bigger surprise than the cupcakes.

Not because Ruby was matchmaking. She loved her kids ferociously, and she was never shy about sticking her nose in other people's business.

But the idea of matching Torey up with somebody like *him*? Or that Torey would ever go along with it?

He knew better, and Ruby should, too. Torey wouldn't have him on a silver platter.

Might as well get this over with. "What do you want, Ruby?" He braced himself for some kind of silliness—which he'd politely refuse to take part in.

"I want you to try to get Torey to give up the Hope Center work and go back to her job in Atlanta."

*"What?"* Stunned, Patrick sank onto the stool next to the phone. "But us running the center together was *your* idea."

"I know. I love that girl beyond all reason, but she's as stubborn as a mud stain. The more I pushed her to go back to Atlanta, the more determined she's been to stay. I figured I'd try a different tack. I don't know if you've noticed, but she ain't too fond of you."

"Yeah." Patrick couldn't decide whether to smile or sigh. "I noticed."

"She angled for that new job for months. I overheard her talking to her boss on the phone this morning, and it was clear that he ain't happy. If she don't get back to work soon, no telling what could happen."

Patrick processed this. It made sense but... "I'm not sure how I can help."

"I'm doing my best to show her I don't need her help here at home. If you show her you don't need her help running the center, then she'll have no reason to stick around."

"But what about all that computer stuff she's starting up? I don't know anything about that."

Ruby made a dismissive noise. "From what I hear, she's got the hard part of that done. Get her to show you the basics of how to run the things, and you'll be all right, I expect."

"Ruby—" Patrick started, but she cut him off.

"I ain't saying you have to be an expert. Just learn enough to get by. And make sure you do your part—the classes and other activities—real well. Show her you got things covered. Torey can't stand feeling useless. If the only person who needs her is that boss in Atlanta, that's where she'll go. Mark my words."

This was the strangest conversation he'd had in a while, which, since he lived with a unicorn-obsessed five-year-old, was saying something. And talking about Torey leaving town made him feel gloomy.

Which made no sense. She'd never really belonged here. No doubt Ruby was right. She'd be better off in Atlanta.

"Okay. I can't promise anything, but I'll do my best."

"Good!" Ruby sounded relieved. "I knew you of all people would understand once I explained things."

*Him of all people.* "Why's that?"

She chuckled. "I'm smarter than I look. I always knew you didn't break up with my girl over that test score business. It was 'cause it showed you how smart she really was and what she'd be giving up if she married you and stayed here. I ain't saying I agreed with your methods, mind. You broke her heart, and I don't take that lightly. But you did it because you believed she was meant for a better life than you could give her. That's easier to forgive."

Patrick couldn't argue because Ruby, as usual, had hit the nail on the head. So, he said nothing.

"Anyhow, I'm obliged to you. Once everybody's back where they need to be, I'll have you over to supper and make you a big pot of chicken and dumplings."

Patrick smiled. Ruby made the best chicken and dumplings in the state of Georgia. He'd savored many a plate of it back when he and Torey were dating. "With corn bread made in your cast-iron skillet?"

"You better believe it."

"I'll hold you to that."

After he hung up the phone, he sat on the stool a minute longer, absently finishing wiping his fingers, his mind lingering on the conversation.

Obviously, Torey was mistaken about the whole matchmaking thing. Ruby wouldn't be enlisting his help to get Torey back to Atlanta if that was the case.

He wasn't surprised she was having trouble getting Torey to leave. Torey didn't give her heart easily, but once she did, she loved with fierce loyalty.

He remembered exactly when he'd learned how fierce that loyalty actually was.

A month before graduation, right in the middle of all the mess with his father, he'd seen a letter from Georgia Tech sitting on Ruby's kitchen table. Opened, the first word clearly visible.

*Congratulations.*

Georgia Tech was Torey's dream school, and he'd been secretly dreading this moment for months. The fallout from his dad's conviction was at its worst, and Torey was the only bright spot in his life. He'd hated the thought of her moving to Atlanta.

But he'd pushed his selfishness aside and waited for her to mention it so they could celebrate. She hadn't said a word. When he'd finally prodded her, Torey had shaken her head.

*I've decided I'll drive over to the community college in Dalton.*

Arguing had gotten him nowhere. Partly because Torey was just too loyal to leave him alone when his life was such a wreck. And partly because he really hadn't tried all that hard.

He'd stayed awake all that night, wrestling with a mixture of guilt and joy. Sometime around dawn, joy had won out.

The next day, he'd taken on a second job so he could buy a diamond ring for the one woman in all the world he knew he could trust. With his heart. With his future.

With everything.

The guilt hadn't gone anywhere, though. It had just bided its time. And later, when Torey had gotten herself into big trouble—because of him—it had pounced.

Patrick blinked, realizing he'd stopped scrubbing and allowed the water to rinse the hand soap uselessly down the drain, leaving his hands dirty.

He scooped out more citrusy soap and started again.

A guy could always get grease stains off his hands if he tried hard enough. Patrick just wished memories could be washed out, too.

It sure would make things simpler.


At two-thirty that afternoon, Torey closed the door to the room at the Hope Center, where she and Patrick were holding their meeting.

And immediately wished she'd left it open.

They were alone in the building, so nobody was going to interrupt them. And since this tiny space did double duty as a storeroom and the director's office, it was cluttered with odds and ends. With Patrick in here, it felt even smaller.

Her normally reliable heart beat a jagged rhythm as she edged past him—why did the man have to have such long legs—and sat in a wobbly office chair. She cleared her throat and readjusted her laptop so that she could see the screen better.

"So," she said, striving to sound calm and competent. "I guess we'd better get started."

"Yeah, we'd better." He glanced at his watch, a simple one that looked like something a grandpa would wear. Patrick wasn't the sort of guy who counted his daily steps. "You go first."

She'd spent most of yesterday preparing for this. She felt strongly about what she was going to say, but she didn't want to be accused of steamrolling over Patrick again.

"I've found some wonderful online opportunities for the kids," she said cautiously. "I'd like us to take advantage of them. Assuming you agree."

He looked suspicious. "What kind of opportunities?"

"I'll show you."

She tapped a few keys on her laptop, bringing up the PowerPoint she'd created. She'd included every reassuring detail she could think of about cybersafety and security, and she'd highlighted a special offer designed for nonprofit organizations like the Hope Center, enabling the kids to take free virtual classes from various schools.

She'd been nervous, but the longer she talked, the more her enthusiasm swelled. When she was growing up in Cedar Ridge, she'd have given anything to have access to technology like this. If Patrick agreed, she could help the current crop of Hope Center kids have the very opportunities she'd longed for.

She loved her ideas so much that her stomach quivered with excitement as she described them. She hadn't felt this enthusiastic for a long time—not even the day she'd started her new job in Atlanta.

Which was a little odd, actually, but she didn't have time to pick apart her feelings right now.

When she finished, she closed the program and looked at Patrick. "So? What do you think?"

"That all sounds good, I guess," he said slowly.

Torey's enthusiasm deflated into disappointment. "These are all excellent opportunities for our kids." Opportunities she'd put a lot of time and effort into finding, thank-you-very-much.

"Our kids." Patrick repeated.

Bad choice of words. He'd once loved to tease her about the kids they might have one day. *If they get your book smarts and my mechanical ability, they'll be unstoppable.*

"I meant the kids the Hope Center serves," she explained stiffly.

"I knew what you meant." He shifted in his chair, looking troubled. "I'm just surprised you're so…invested. I thought for you this was about keeping Ruby happy."

"Well, it is. Mostly. But I can empathize with these kids. I didn't have the easiest time growing up myself, and I'd genuinely like to help them if I can."

Patrick seemed to be thinking that over. "Fair enough. Okay. I'll agree, on two conditions."

"What conditions?"

"First off, that you teach me some computer stuff."

For a full ten seconds Torey couldn't do anything but stare at him.

"Teach you. About computers." She got the words out finally.

"Right."

Torey leaned back in the chair, which squawked a warning. "Are you ser—"

The rickety chair collapsed, tumbling her onto the floor. As she fell, she bumped the metal shelving against the back wall, provoking an avalanche of art supplies. Faded construction paper, glue sticks and fabric scraps rained over her.

Patrick was at her side in a second, brushing the debris off her. "Are you okay?"

"I think so." He helped her up, his strong hands

closing gently over her arms, and her stomach fluttered. She glared at the chair, twisted on the floor. "That's going to the dumpster."

Patrick nudged it with a boot. "Maybe. I'll take a look and see if I can fix it. In the meantime, I'll bring in another chair." He looked at the junk scattered across the floor and shook his head. "Looks like we'll need some trash bags, too."

"Definitely. Cleaning out this office just got bumped up on my to-do list." They were standing too close together. She edged backward, perching on the edge of the desk. "Sorry. So you were… um…saying you want me to help you learn about computers?" She still wasn't sure she'd heard him right.

"I think that would be a good idea, yeah." He plucked a scrap of yellow paper from her hair, and the light touch made the butterflies in her stomach ramp up a notch.

She swallowed. "I didn't think you liked computers."

"I don't," he said flatly. "But I have a foster son who does, so I need to figure them out, best I can. Plus, when you go back to Atlanta, I'll still be here. It'll probably help the new director if I have some idea of how all the techy stuff works."

That made sense. She should have suggested it herself. Maybe she would have if she'd had any idea that Patrick would agree to it.

Having him suggest it out of the blue like this had thrown her for a loop.

"Okay. Well, I'll be happy to walk you through everything. And you can sit in when the kids are doing computer activities to see what's going on, if you'd like to."

His nose wrinkled, but he gave a resigned nod. "Fine."

"And of course, we won't only offer computer-based activities. If you have any ideas about other stuff the kids can do, I'm all ears. But if you haven't had time to think about it—"

"Actually, I have." Patrick reached into his shirt pocket and produced a square of paper. He unfolded it carefully and handed it to her.

Torey scanned the brightly colored flyer. It was an information sheet for Cedar Ridge's Harvest Celebration parade, outlining the requirements for participation and guidelines for float construction.

"Wow." She lifted her eyebrows. "I didn't even know this was still going on."

"Every year. It's a tradition."

"Right. It's just…the last time I saw the parade about six years ago, it seemed a little…" She trailed off, searching for the right word. Moth-eaten. Bedraggled. "Tired," she said tactfully.

"Maybe we can help re-energize it."

"Uh-huh." She glanced back at the paper in her

hand. "So, you want the Hope Center to enter a float?"

"I do." He leaned forward, his blue eyes sparkling with intensity. "Think about it. It's got something for everybody. There's the design of it, the mechanics—our float could have moving parts. We could use lawn mower engines, things like that, to make the different pieces work. I could help the kids build them. Here." He pulled a second bit of paper out of his shirt pocket. "I planned out a rough schedule for a beginner's engine class. If it's okay by you, I'll have the schools announce it so we can get kids signed up."

He was really well prepared. "What about the kids who aren't interested in engines?"

"They can work on the decorations for the float. I spoke with the art teacher at Jill's school. She'd be happy to teach an arts and crafts class here twice a week. And if the kids wanted to wear costumes, maybe your sister-in-law Charlotte could help. She designs clothes, doesn't she?"

"She does." And she'd be willing to help out, Torey was sure.

Okay, she was impressed. Maybe the guy didn't have a PowerPoint, but he'd definitely thought this through.

"At the parade, some of the kids could walk alongside the float, handing out candy, and some could ride. I thought maybe Ruby might like to be on the float, too, since she's one of the founders of the Hope Center. If you think she's up to it."

"Oh!" Torey smiled. Ruby riding on a float with her beloved Hope Center kids. "I think she'd love that."

Patrick smiled, and Torey's heart did another silly dip and roll. "All the kids'll probably want to ride, so I figure I'll set up some kind of reward system to earn a spot. That might encourage them to work on behaving themselves better. They can earn points, and I'll pick a certain number from each age group. Once the parade's over, we can pick some other rewards for them to work toward."

Torey tried to sort out her thoughts. "How would they earn the points?"

"Lots of ways." Patrick took the flyer from Torey's hand, flipping it over. As he did, their fingers brushed, and her heart did another tap dance. This was getting ridiculous. "I wrote some ideas down. Staying out of trouble at school. Taking a life skills class here. Helping construct the float, helping with center cleanup or odd jobs. Tutoring a younger kid or helping them with homework. That kind of thing. Plus, they could take part in some fun outdoor activities, too. Jorgeson's Farm is doing their usual corn maze and pumpkin picking thing this year. I spoke with them, and they said they'd discount the group price for the Hope Center. They offered a really good deal."

"I'm not surprised. The Jorgesons are great people." Her youngest foster sister had worked there all during high school.

"Jina used to work there, didn't she?"

"She still helps out at the farm when she's in town." She hesitated. "I almost hate to take the discount. Jorgeson's has been struggling. It used to be a popular local field trip destination in the fall, but lately there just hasn't been that much interest."

Patrick seemed undeterred. "All the more reason to take the kids there. Maybe they'll enjoy it and spread the word. Jorgeson's has been a fixture in Cedar Ridge for thirty years. It'd be a shame for it to close."

Yes, it would. But that didn't change the facts. She searched for a polite way to pose her question. "And you think the kids will want to do these things?"

He leaned back in his chair, looking surprised. "What kid wouldn't?"

Torey decided to be honest. "Probably a lot of them. Parades and farm trips are fun, but kids have sophisticated tastes nowadays."

"Deep down, kids are still kids," Patrick said. "They haven't changed as much as people think."

Torey jiggled her knee as she considered this. She had nothing against small-town parades, and she liked the idea of helping the Jorgesons. The family had been kind and understanding to her sister when Jina had struggled with anxiety. That counted for a lot in Torey's book.

"All right," she decided. "I appreciate your taking the time to put all these ideas together. Let's try it. We'll balance out the computer activities with the ones you're suggesting and see how it goes." She set her computer on her lap and got ready to take notes. "We've got a lot of work to do. Let's get it all planned out so we can get things started."

"Don't worry about that," Patrick said. "I can handle everything."

She looked up and frowned. "This is going to be a lot of work. And as you reminded me earlier, we're codirectors, so we cooperate." She paused. "Or does that rule only run one way?"

Patrick looked uncomfortable. "Well, no. I guess it doesn't."

An explanation occurred to her—along with a twinge of guilt. "Don't worry. I won't try to take over. I promise." She angled Patrick's papers beside her on the desk, her fingers flying over the keyboard. "Your kids will be out of school soon, so let's set up a class schedule and get the reward system hammered out. If we can get the Hope Center running smoothly, I'm sure that'll make it easier for the board to hire a new director."

"You're right." Patrick looked relieved. "I guess you're anxious to get back home."

"I'm in no hurry," she murmured, squinting at

the screen. "Ryder and Elise and their boys are visiting Ruby today."

"I wasn't talking about Ruby's house. I meant your real home. Atlanta. You must really miss it."

"Oh." Torey's fingers stilled, her mind flashing to her apartment. One bedroom, a galley kitchen, and a drawer full of takeout menus. Perfect for her.

But she'd never considered it home.

She remembered Patrick's house—the big, fenced yard, the comfortable clutter, the feeling of family.

"Torey?"

Patrick was still waiting for an answer.

"Absolutely," she said. "I need to get back to Atlanta as soon as I can."

He nodded. "That's what I thought." He scooted his chair a little closer. "Okay. We'll work together, then. The sooner we get the center on its feet, the better."

# Chapter Five

A week and a half later, Patrick walked around his classroom at the Hope Center, supervising the very first Engines for Beginners class. His students weren't the only beginners in the room. He'd never taught before, but so far so good.

He and Torey had been working round the clock since their meeting, getting the center spruced up and open for business. The place still wasn't perfect, but it was functional, and they'd reopened a couple of days ago, welcoming a modest number of students. Not too shabby, all things considered.

Now he just had to hold up his end of things. He was scheduled to teach two classes, a high school auto maintenance class and this one, aimed at younger students.

Right now, a dozen kids aged eight to twelve were disassembling six lawn mower motors, positioned on plastic tarps. They'd take the things apart and put them back together first. Then they'd adapt them for whatever whirligigs the float needed.

As Patrick leaned over to inspect one of the engines, his phone buzzed in his pocket. Again. He ignored it. Again.

These kids deserved his full attention. Besides, he was having fun, and he didn't want to miss a minute.

He halted here and there, offering advice or praise and answering the occasional question, but all the kids seemed busy and happy.

Well, all but one.

Patrick watched Josh from the corner of his eye. He knelt beside a motor, watching his partner industriously spinning a screwdriver. Josh looked bored out of his mind, and Patrick smothered a sigh.

Josh hadn't been thrilled about taking this class, but the only other one offered at this time was Sadie's art class, and Jill was in that one. Josh loved his little sister, but he didn't want to spend an hour doing arts and crafts with elementary school kids.

He didn't want to be here, either, but since Patrick was teaching, Josh was stuck at the center.

As he watched, Josh's eyes darted to the clock, and his expression brightened. Only fifteen minutes before he'd get to spend time in Torey's new computer lab. Ever since the Hope Center had reopened—and his screen suspension had lifted—it was the only place Josh wanted to be.

Patrick wished the kid would show a little interest in something else—something they could share.

"Remember," he said, carefully not looking in Josh's direction as he spoke, "in this class we're learning basic skills. Most of you won't become professional mechanics like me, but you'll drive cars, right?"

There was a murmur of agreement.

"Well, if you know your way around an engine, you can save yourself a lot of money."

"I'd rather just pay somebody to fix my car," Josh muttered.

"I'm sure glad people pay me, but it helps if you know a little something yourself. That way you're less likely to get cheated by a dishonest mechanic."

He winced as soon as the words left his mouth. Seeing as how his own family members were some of the most dishonest mechanics in Georgia, that probably wasn't the best thing to bring up. Happily, none of the kids seemed to notice.

"It's four thirty," Josh announced. "Class is s'posed to be over." The collective groan from the other kids made Patrick smile.

"Throw the ends of your tarp over your engine, making sure you've got all the parts you've taken off tucked inside. We'll finish this up next time."

Josh was already halfway to the door. "Hey," Patrick called. "You can't leave your partner to clean up alone. Do your part, son."

Grudgingly Josh returned and quickly helped the other boy follow Patrick's instructions. But he still managed to be first out the door, no doubt making a beeline to his favorite station in Torey's lab.

Patrick battled disappointment as he dragged the engines out of the middle of the floor and lined them against the wall. This class had been a good idea, he told himself. Lawn mower engines were small and easy for kids to work with. He'd removed all sharp parts, and as he'd suspected, the kids had loved the chance to use real tools. Nothing taught you more about an engine—in Patrick's opinion—than taking one apart and putting it back together.

He just wished Josh had enjoyed it. He needed to connect with the boy, and he was running low on ideas. He had one more family-building trick up his sleeve, planned for next Saturday. He sure hoped it worked.

If it didn't, he wasn't sure what he was going to do.

Everything Patrick was good at—engines, fishing, home repairs, gardening—Josh couldn't care less about. And the stuff Josh liked—computers and video games—Patrick knew next to nothing about.

Which reminded him, he needed to get to the computer lab so he could sit in on Torey's lesson. For one thing, he'd promised Ruby, and he'd like to keep some of his word, anyway. Torey was proving as stubborn as her mom had predicted, insisting on being in the middle of all the non-computer activities, so he was already blowing that part.

Also, there was a chance—a slight one—that he might at least learn enough to keep Josh out of trouble.

So far Josh's teachers hadn't reported any more problems with his behavior. But as Patrick scooted the last swaddled engine in place, he frowned, recalling that insistently buzzing phone.

He'd better check and see who'd been so persistent. It was after school hours, but he'd made it clear that the teachers could call him at any time. He pulled out his phone and navigated his way back to his missed calls.

It was an unknown number. Might be spam, might be one of his customers. A few of his best ones had this number in addition to the landline at his shop. And it might be one of Josh's teachers, if they'd called from a personal phone. Whoever it was wasn't in his contacts, so he couldn't be sure.

They'd called three times. He didn't want to miss a call from a teacher. And he sure didn't need word getting back to Mitzi that he was blowing off calls about Josh's behavior.

He hit the button to return the call and waited while it rang. He didn't have to wait long.

"Hello?" A man's voice, gravelly and familiar. Patrick frowned.

"This is Patrick Callahan," he said. "Looks like I missed a few calls from this number. Have you been trying to reach me?"

An uneasy chuckle came through the line. "I sure have." Short pause. "Hello there, son."

Patrick's hand tightened around the phone. "Dad?"

"That's right." A soft cough. "You're a hard fellow to get hold of."

Patrick's shock hardened into wariness. "I'm really busy these days."

"I won't take much of your time," Ron Callahan promised quickly. "I'd just like to talk to you, Patrick. Maybe go to supper or something." A pause. "I've been doing real good since I got out."

His dad sounded...lonely. And older. Patrick did some quick calculations in his head. How long had he been out of prison? Maybe four years? Five? Something like that. He'd be well up in his sixties now.

But still. The last time his dad had called, "doing good" and wanting a reunion, Patrick had given in and invited him to come to the garage. Cars had always been the only thing they'd ever had in common, so he'd figured that would be the least uncomfortable spot for their meet up.

But Ron hadn't come alone. He'd shown up with one of Patrick's cousins, and two days after their visit, Callahan's Motors had been broken into. A rare part—the supercharger off a client's '57 Thunderbird engine—had gone missing. It was easily the most valuable item in the shop at the time, something only a car connoisseur would have known. Ron's number had been disconnected, so Patrick had been forced to call the police. An identical part had resurfaced on a shady online resale site two weeks later, and Patrick had ended up having an uncomfortable chat with law enforcement about it.

The officials had finally backed off. They were obviously not convinced Patrick wasn't involved, but since they couldn't produce any evidence, they'd finally stopped asking questions. Thankfully, the client had been appeased by Patrick's willingness to replace the hard-to-find part—at his personal expense—and to discount his work on the car restoration because of the "inconvenience."

That incident had toppled Patrick's precarious budget into the red, splashed mud on a reputation he'd worked hard to clean up, and served as a painful reminder of why he'd cut ties with his family in the first place.

Right now, he had a garage full of expensive cars with all kinds of rare and pricey parts. No

way he could let his sticky-fingered relatives anywhere near that.

That included his father.

Patrick cleared his throat. He hated what he
was about to do. But he had Josh and Jill to look
after, and a social worker who already had her
doubts about him. The more distance he kept between himself and his train wreck of a family—
all of them—the better.

The Callahan clan had already destroyed his
hopes for a family once. He couldn't let that happen again.

"Sorry, Dad. Like I said, I'm busy these days.
I'm glad things are good with you, though. I wish
you well."

"Patrick—" He heard the pleading desperation in his father's voice just before he disconnected the call.

He stood in the empty room, listening to the
muffled sounds of children's voices. Two of those
kids were his…for now. And if he could get into
Mitzi's good graces, maybe forever. He wasn't
willing to risk that just because his father happened to be feeling lonely.

Or, Patrick reflected as he turned off the lights
in his classroom, more likely, happened to be
short of cash. Which brought up another problem he'd better deal with.

He'd have to let Torey know he'd be missing

class today. He needed to double-check his garage's security system.

Knowing his family, it was probably about to get a workout.

Torey surveyed her buzzing kingdom with satisfaction. The Hope Center's new computer lab was a huge success. The kids were busily involved in a variety of high-level educational programs—carefully curated by her brother-in-law Neil, a teacher at the local high school.

He'd been happy to help out. The school's budget didn't run to new equipment, so he agreed with her that this was a great opportunity for local students.

She strolled through the room, glancing at the monitors and assisting the kids who needed help. A lot of them did. Most had never had access to computers this new or programs this well designed.

But they did now. She'd been unprepared for how happy that made her.

It wasn't really about the computers she'd convinced friends and colleagues to donate. It was about the expressions on the kids' faces—the joy and the awe as they discovered the marvels at their fingertips. She'd opened up a new world for them, and she prayed she'd managed to knock down some of the obstacles the world had set in front of them.

A fierce joy thrummed through her body, and the only sliver of unhappiness was the realization that this was all temporary.

For her, she reminded herself. It was temporary for her. These computers would be available for the children to use even after she'd gone, and that was what mattered.

Still, the idea of leaving her lab behind in somebody else's hands felt itchy and uncomfortable, like a scratchy sweater.

She'd been thinking about that a good bit lately.

She'd planned to stay here her full three months. That length of family leave was written into her contract, although she knew her boss hadn't expected her to be taking advantage of it so soon. But Ruby had needed her, so Torey hadn't thought twice.

Which was fine if Ruby truly did need her. She had, at first, but now, Torey wasn't so sure. This morning, she'd discovered her foster mom in the kitchen making biscuits before dawn, looking as spry as her old self. She'd waved off Torey's offers to help and shooed her out the back door with her dishcloth—after reminding her that the Hope Center board would be putting another advertisement online for a permanent director.

Then there'd been Patrick's offer to handle the center's involvement in the parade on his own. He'd backed down when she'd insisted, but clearly, he didn't want her help any more than Ruby did.

Add in the snippy impatience in her boss's emails, and she should probably start making plans to move back to Atlanta.

Back *home*, she amended firmly. Where she belonged.

And she would. Soon. But not yet, she decided with a guilty sense of relief. It was still early days with the center, and there was a lot left to do. And whether or not Patrick wanted her help, she intended to do her share. Until she did officially step away, the Hope Center was half her responsibility. Torey had suffered at the hands of too many irresponsible people not to take her own obligations seriously.

Patrick came out of his classroom and beckoned to her, interrupting her thoughts. She stepped through her door and stood just outside it where she could still keep an eye on the kids.

"Listen," Patrick said. "I'll have to bow out of my computer lesson today. I need to run to the garage. It won't take long, and I'll be right back to pick up Jill and Josh. Okay?"

"Sure." She frowned, noticing worry lines etched across his forehead. "Something wrong?"

"I just need to check on something. If you don't mind, I'd like to let my kids know I'm leaving." Patrick looked over her shoulder and scanned the lab, zeroing in on Josh. The boy was seated in the back row seat he'd claimed the first time Torey had opened the doors, and he appeared totally intent on his screen.

"Of course." Torey understood why Patrick wouldn't just slip away. Foster kids had generally weathered a lot of unpredictability in their lives. It was a good idea to be as consistent as possible with them, giving them a heads up about any change in routine. "I can tell him if you want."

"No, I'll do it." Patrick hesitated. "He sure looks interested."

He sounded a little down, and Torey's heart panged with sympathy. She'd seen how Josh had raced out of Patrick's classroom and how excited he'd been to snag his favorite station. Clearly Josh didn't share his foster dad's distrust of technology—or his fascination with engines.

"They all are," she pointed out. "This is new and exciting. Some of that will wear off in time."

"I'm not sure it will with Josh. Computers are all he seems to care about. Well, that and Jill."

Torey didn't answer. There wasn't anything she could say that would be helpful. Her fascination with computers certainly hadn't worn off, and Josh was as passionate about them as she'd been at his age.

She followed Patrick as he threaded his way through the computer stations until he reached his foster son.

"Josh." He spoke softly, but the boy jumped, startled. "I've got to run to the garage, but—"

"Whoa," Torey interrupted, leaning forward. "What are you doing?" The boy's fingers scrabbled to close the computer window, but not before she recognized what was on the screen. Her mouth drooped open with astonishment.

*"Warriors of Kadan.* Josh—"

"Isn't that the game you said wasn't allowed? What's he doing playing it?" Patrick sounded both confused and alarmed.

"It's not allowed," she confirmed. "And we've installed safeguards restricting games with questionable content." Josh's cheeks were bright red, and he was avoiding her gaze. "Or we thought we had. How'd you get past them?"

Josh's eyes were wide. "I…uh…just did. It wasn't hard—and honest, this game ain't that bad. You should play it yourself and see."

Nice try. But nope. "I did my homework" she informed him. "Its rating is well deserved for the violence alone. And that's not the only issue."

"But—"

"The point is, Miss Torey said it was off-limits." Patrick cut in, his eyes like blue-green ice. "Which you knew when you went around the—" he gestured at the computer "—guardrails or whatever. You can't keep doing that, Josh."

Torey was suddenly aware of all the kids watching them.

"We'll talk about this later—and privately," she murmured, tapping the power button on the computer. "In the meantime, Josh's lab time is finished for the day."

Josh groaned, and Torey saw Patrick's jaw firm. "Yeah, well, you should've thought of that before you pulled another stunt. Come on. I've got to go to the garage, and it looks like you're coming with me."

"When you come back to pick up Jill, we can talk," Torey said. "And Josh, I'm going to have some questions for you." She needed to know exactly how the kid had pulled this off so she could make sure it never happened again.

"I think I'll take Jill with me, too," Patrick said. "Her art class is over anyway. The teacher was just letting her stay and draw until Josh's class was done."

"But—"

"If you want to talk this over, come to the house tonight after supper," Patrick interrupted. "Grab your stuff, Josh, and let's go."

Josh stood up slowly and snagged his book bag from the corner. He kept his head ducked down, and he looked miserable. "Miss Torey? I'm—I'm really sorry."

The wobble in the kid's voice softened her heart. It wasn't as if she'd never made a mistake like this herself. She had—and a much bigger one. Sometimes when you knew how to get around a rule, temptation was hard to resist.

And as she knew all too well, the consequences could break your heart.

"I'm sorry, too, Josh," she said.

And she was, she thought, watching Patrick and Josh head toward the art classroom to collect Jill. This incident was only going to make Patrick more convinced that his foster son needed less screen time.

If she was right about Josh's passion for computers, that attitude would likely drive a bigger wedge between a troubled kid and the one guy in the whole world who was genuinely trying to help him.

Torey tightened her lips. She shouldn't meddle. She really shouldn't.

But she already knew she was going to.

# Chapter Six

"The kids are in the kitchen." Patrick motioned Torey inside the house. "Do you want to talk to me first or to Josh?"

Torey swallowed. This—driving to her former fiancé's home, sweaty, nervous, and guilty—was starting to feel way too familiar.

She wanted to smooth things over and—if she saw an opportunity—see if she could shift Patrick's opinions a little where Josh and computers were concerned.

That wouldn't be easy, so better start with the apology.

She cleared her throat. "There's not much I can say to you, except that every precaution was taken to make sure nothing inappropriate was allowed on those computers. I'm sorry this happened, and I'm looking into beefing up our safeguards."

Patrick didn't appear impressed. "I'm not blaming you, Torey. Josh has found his way around stuff like that before. But I'm guessing there's no guarantee this won't happen again. Right?"

She couldn't blame him for asking the question. "Well, no. But I think it's unlikely."

Patrick nodded, but he didn't seem reassured. "Kitchen's this way," he said, leading the way down a hallway.

Josh and Jill looked up as she and Patrick walked into the room. The kids were seated at the table, the remains of their dinner in front of them. Half of a chicken potpie in a disposable foil pan, flanked by a bowl of salad and fluffy biscuits that looked like somebody's grandma had made them.

The whole kitchen had a grandma feel. It sported red and white checkered curtains at the windows, an enamel-topped table with matching red trim and fat little canisters on the counter masquerading as potbellied pigs wearing chef's hats.

It was as different from her chrome and black apartment kitchen as night and day, but oddly enough, Torey liked it. It was cute in a retro kind of way, and it felt comforting and homey. It reminded her of Ruby's kitchen, the kind of old-fashioned room where families sat down to eat a nice supper and talk about their day.

"You guys done?" Patrick asked.

Jilly nodded. "Yes, and I ate all my green beans. Can I have a cookie now?"

He tousled the little girl's hair. It was pulled back in barrettes today, and one was slipping loose. "You sure can. Tell you what, Jillybean. Let's take your cookie into the family room and I'll turn on that princess movie you like, okay? Miss Torey and I need to talk to Josh for a minute."

Jill's small face clouded, and she cast a concerned look at her brother.

"Go on," Josh ordered gruffly. "Better watch that girlie movie while you can, 'cause when I get in there, I'm gonna want to watch something else."

"Okay," she agreed softly. She waited while Patrick retrieved a large cookie from an Angelo's bakery box. As the little girl followed him to the door, she reached up for his hand, her little fingers twining naturally with his.

Torey watched them, her heart turning backflips in her chest. Patrick looked so natural with the kids—no surprise there. He was born to be a dad. She was surprised he hadn't married and had half a dozen kids by now.

For years she'd held her breath whenever his name had come up, expecting to hear about an engagement or a wedding—and determined not to care when she did. But that had never happened.

Since for whatever reason he'd never married, she gave him big points for stepping up to foster. She and her siblings knew what a difference a good foster parent could make.

She and Patrick might not see eye to eye on some things—okay, several things—but he was, in many ways, the same guy she'd once fallen head over heels for.

She'd been wondering if she'd exaggerated Patrick's good qualities in her memory because none of the men she'd gone out with since had measured up. Those relationships had fizzled fast, and she'd never come close to feeling about any of them the way she'd felt about Patrick.

Surely, she must have colored up her memories with the glow of a first love and all the innocence and optimism that came with that. No guy was as kind and good-hearted as the Patrick she remembered. She'd even thought that spending this time with him might fix that—giving her an overdue dose of reality.

But watching him with these kids… Well, it wasn't helping.

"So? We gonna talk or what?" Josh looked at her, his expression a mixture of defiance and shame.

"Yes," she agreed immediately. "We are. You want to go first?"

"Okay." Josh ducked his head. "I'm sorry I played *Warriors of Kadan* at the Hope Center."

Torey lifted an eyebrow and gave the kid points for the apology. But then he went on.

"It ain't that bad a game, though. Everybody's playing it at school."

Torey managed to stop her grin just in time. Nice try. She attempted the same "everybody's doing it" argument with Ruby when she was a teenager. It hadn't worked.

"That's not the point." She pulled out a chair, sat down and helped herself to a biscuit. "The point is, you knew that game was off-limits. And you went to a lot of trouble to get around all the safeguards to download it." She broke the biscuit open and reached for the butter. "By the way, how'd you do that?"

She kept the question casual and didn't glance Josh's way as she spoke. Out of the corner of her eye, she saw him shrug.

"It wasn't hard. Are you—am I getting kicked out of computer lab?"

Torey was buttering her biscuit, but she paused in midsmear. The kid's voice was shaking. He was truly worried.

"What do you think?"

He swallowed. "I guess I deserve it. But please give me another chance." Josh went on desperately. "I know I did the wrong thing, and I'll never do that again. If you'll let me keep coming to lab, I'll do anything you want, okay? I'll—" he gestured frantically "—I'll clean the place up. I'll help the little kids. I'll do whatever it takes. Computer stuff…" His voice broke. "It's the only thing in the whole world I'm any good at."

Torey blinked. That sounded awfully familiar.

Josh was waiting for her answer, his body tense as if he was expecting a blow. She chewed slowly, although the biscuit had turned to sawdust in her mouth.

*Whew.* This was tough. She was more convinced than ever that she needed to talk to Patrick, but she still didn't think he'd be willing to listen.

"I appreciate your apology and your promises, Josh, but this isn't only my decision to make."

"What isn't only your decision?" Patrick spoke from the doorway.

She took a breath. It was now or never. "Josh, Patrick and I need to talk privately. Okay?"

She tried to keep her tone stern and neutral, but she must not have done too good a job. Hope sparked into Josh's eyes.

"Yeah! Sure!" Pushing back his chair, he jumped to his feet. "I'll go in the living room with Jill." Halfway to the door, he turned, looking awkward and desperate. "Paddy, listen. If you let me keep using the lab, I won't do nothing like this ever again, okay? You got my word."

Patrick's face softened as he studied the boy. "We'll talk it over, Josh," was all he said. "Shut the door on your way out."

The boy threw Torey a last pleading look before he pulled the door closed.

"So." Torey stalled for time to think. "The kids call you by your old football nickname?"

"Jill does." Patrick looked embarrassed. "That's actually the first time Josh has called me that. He thinks it's dumb. And maybe it is. It's hard, figuring out what they should call you. Paddy sounds silly, maybe, but I'd rather be goofy than stand-offish. And it's pretty close to Daddy if—" He paused and shrugged. "If this turns out to be permanent," he finished.

Torey's eyes widened. "You're planning to adopt them?" That was huge news. Most foster kids ended up returning to their birth parents or aging out of care.

"If I can," Patrick said. "Reunification isn't an option for them."

"And as their foster parent, you'll be given priority."

"I'm hoping so. The social worker isn't thrilled about the trouble Josh has been getting into at school. My biggest problem with Jill is figuring out how to do her hair. But Josh is really struggling."

"Well," Torey said carefully, "that's to be expected, isn't it? He's only been with you, what? A few months? It took all of us a lot longer than that to settle down with Ruby, and she was a pro."

She winced. Maybe pointing out Patrick's inexperience wasn't so tactful. But he didn't seem offended.

"Mitzi believes Josh's acting out is proof this placement isn't working." He raked a hand through his hair. "I'm trying to help Josh behave, but nothing seems to do much good. I just can't find a way to connect with him."

Yeah." Torey nodded slowly. "He doesn't seem too interested in cars."

"No. Or football, or fishing. Or anything I know anything about. I've tried everything I can think of, but going by what happened today, I'm not making much progress."

Torey nibbled the biscuit she'd snitched, unsure how to respond. She'd led off with an apology for what had happened at the center, but it didn't sound like Patrick was blaming her at all.

He was blaming himself.

"Did you make these biscuits?" she asked suddenly.

Patrick seemed surprised at the change of topic. "Yeah. When I started the foster training, I got a cookbook and started practicing. While I was on my own, I ate mostly takeout and boxed stuff, but kids need homemade food."

Torey's imagination presented her with an image of Patrick doggedly trying recipes out of a cookbook for the sake of kids he'd not even met yet.

She tried unsuccessfully to swallow the lump that formed in her throat.

"Well, they're really good," she said. "Not as good as Ruby's, but close."

One corner of Patrick's mouth tipped up. "That's high praise."

"It's sincere."

"Thanks. I've figured out biscuits and a few other things. But—" he nodded at the half-eaten pot pie "—a lot of our food still comes straight from the supermarket's freezer section." He shook his head. "I don't know. Maybe Mitzi's right."

"Mitzi's wrong," Torey told him. "Anybody can see that you're giving this parenting thing a hundred percent, and that's more than good enough. I mean, look at this place." She gestured around kitchen. "Red-checkered curtains, a white picket fence. A refrigerator with the kid's photos and drawings on it. You're a big, goofy dog and a nosy neighbor away from living in an old sitcom. Josh is only acting out because that's what kids do when their lives feel out of control. He'll settle down."

Patrick rubbed his forehead. "If that doesn't happen soon, his life could go right off the rails."

Torey shot Patrick a measuring look, wondering if he'd be willing to hear her out. "You know," she ventured, "before you came back, I was talking to Josh about what happened. He's worried that he's going to be banned from the computer lab."

Patrick's brow furrowed. "Shouldn't he be?"

"I'm not so sure." She tried to think of how best to approach this touchy subject. "Remember when we were in high school, how you used to say that fixing cars was the only thing you were ever good at?"

He studied her, his expression wary. "Yeah."

"Josh said something similar to me, that computer stuff is the only thing he's good at."

"That's not true," Patrick protested. "He's a smart kid, and he's good at lots of things. Or he could be. He's just not interested in anything else."

"People could've said the same thing about me. Or about you. And imagine how you'd have felt if somebody had cut you off from cars altogether. And," she went on relentlessly, "that could've happened. I mean, after your dad got into trouble. Somebody could have thought—better keep this kid away from the garage or he'll turn out just like his father."

Patrick's silence made her heart pound. She was treading on dangerously thin ice. Patrick's family was a very sore subject.

"This," he said finally, "is different."

"I don't think it is, Patrick. Computers are what Josh feels good at, and honestly? He *is* good at them. All my techy friends are amazed that he found a way around all the protections we had in place to get to that game. That's not low-level stuff. This kid has serious talent."

Patrick rose and started clearing away the dishes. "My dad and my cousins have talent, too.

Talent isn't what matters. It's how you use it that counts."

"Exactly," she agreed. "That's why you should make sure Josh has an outlet for his. If you try to shut this off, trust me, he's going to find a way to use it anyway."

Torey stood up. She'd spent too long in Ruby's household to watch somebody clear away dishes without offering to help. Since she knew Patrick would just refuse the offer, she didn't make it. She simply stacked up the plates and carried them to the sink, Patrick shot her a surprised look, but he didn't protest.

"I'm not saying there shouldn't be consequences," Torey went on. "Just maybe don't try to keep him off computers too long. You have any tinfoil? I'll cover the rest of this potpie."

Patrick reached under the sink and wordlessly handed her a box of foil.

They worked in silence for a few minutes, and as they did, the funny tickling in Torey's stomach intensified.

She wasn't sure what was getting to her. Maybe Patrick's silence? Because nothing special was going on.

There was only the clatter of plates, the quiet, homey acts of wiping crumbs off a table and stowing leftovers in the fridge. The lingering smells of food and the sight of Patrick with a dish towel slung over one broad shoulder, as he scraped and rinsed the dishes before stacking them in the dishwasher. The bright sounds of a children's movie filtered in from the living room, punctuated by a trill of delighted laughter from Jill.

"Josh must not have followed through on his threat to make her turn off that movie," Torey said.

"He never does," Patrick said, one corner of his mouth tipping up. He glanced at her, and their eyes met.

"He's a good kid," Torey pointed out quietly.

"Yeah," Patrick agreed. "He is a good kid." He nodded at the door with a tired grin. "He's also a sneaky kid. Come on in. I know you're out there."

Josh opened the door and peered in. His face was so pale that all his freckles stood out. She wondered how long he'd been listening.

Patrick sucked in a slow breath. "Okay, Josh," he said. "Three weeks. Three weeks with no screens at home or at the Center."

"Three *weeks*?" Josh groaned.

"It could be shortened," Patrick said. "If you meet a few conditions."

"What conditions?"

"I've planned some stuff for us to do during those three weeks, here at home and at the center. Non-computer stuff. If you go along with a good attitude, maybe we can shorten that time to two weeks."

"Is she coming, too?" Josh nodded at Torey. "To do all the dumb stuff." The boy caught sight of Patrick's expression. "I mean, the other stuff? Miss Torey, will you?"

The question took Torey by surprise—and so did the half-shy, half-anxious look on Josh's face. He was obviously hoping she'd say yes.

"Torey's pretty busy," Patrick said quickly. "She's taking care of Mrs. Ruby and helping out with the Hope Center, too, remember."

Josh's face fell. "Yeah," he muttered. "And working in the computer lab's a lot more fun anyhow."

Torey looked from Patrick's face to Josh's. "I have time."

"Really?" Josh's face brightened.

"Sure." She'd promised to help with the parade activities anyway, she told herself. 'I know something about what your—uh—Paddy's got planned, and it's going to be a lot of fun. I wouldn't miss it."

"Not just the center stuff? The home stuff, too?"

"Josh, we can't ask Torey to give up all her time," Patrick stated firmly, and the hope in the boy's face ebbed.

"Why not?" Torey asked coolly, and the boy's eyes lit back up. "I like to have fun as much as the next person. Count me in."

"Great! Count me in, too, then."

"Good," Patrick said after a minute. "Well, when two men strike a bargain, they shake on it." He held out one hand. The boy regarded him warily, then straightened his skinny shoulders and stuck his own hand out. As they shook, Torey's eyes started stinging.

She turned away, pretending to fuss with wringing out the dishcloth Patrick had been using. This, she thought desperately, was ridiculous. She wasn't like her foster sisters, who cried at the drop of a hat. She never had been.

But this—well, it brought up a memory of one of those rare moments when her own life had balanced on a thread, when she made a choice that ended up changing everything.

When she'd come to live at Ruby's, the older woman had sat her down and talked to her like she was a grown-up. She'd laid out the rules and made Torey some promises—promises sixteen-year-old Torey was much too jaded to believe in.

In her experience, adults didn't keep their word. Her mom hadn't, her social worker hadn't and neither had any of the foster parents she'd had before now. She saw no reason why this old woman would be any different.

As if Ruby understood that, she'd stuck her bony hand out and suggested they shake on their deal.

Something about that firm handshake and the no-nonsense way Ruby had looked into her eyes had reached the last hopeful spot in Torey's calloused heart. She'd decided she'd give this old lady a chance.

Just one.

One was all Ruby had needed. And after that—not right away, but slowly, over time—everything in Torey's life had changed for the better. She hoped—she really hoped—that the same thing would happen for Josh now.

She felt a tap on her elbow and turned to find Josh looking up at her. "I want to shake on it with you, too, Miss Torey. I won't mess up in the computer lab ever again."

She made herself smile. "Deal. And in three weeks, I'll hold you to that promise."

A determined glint sparkled in Josh's eyes. "Two weeks," he tossed over his shoulder as he left the kitchen.

"Starting now," Patrick called after him.

"I think that went well." Torey kept her tone light and casual.

"Thanks to you." Patrick looked at her, and something in his eyes made the tickle in her stomach intensify. "I didn't mean for you to get roped in. I tried to give you an out." He paused. "You didn't take it."

No, she hadn't. And she wasn't entirely sure why.

"Seriously, though, thanks. Apart from computers, getting you to come along is the first thing

Josh has shown any interest in. So, I appreciate it. Although," he added, as if to himself, "I don't know what Ruby'll have to say."

"Don't worry about Ruby," she said, "She's doing a lot better, and she'll probably be relieved to have me out from under her feet."

Patrick studied her, his expression unreadable. "Maybe you're right."

"So." She folded the dishcloth over the faucet and pretended indifference. "When do I need to report for duty?"

Patrick thought it over for a minute. "Saturday afternoon. Say around two? Wear jeans and a shirt you don't mind getting dirty. I think I'm going to take your advice."

She frowned. "What advice?"

He grinned and leaned in so close that the scent of oranges mingled with the homey kitchen smells of dishwashing detergent and chicken pot-pie.

"You see, the thing is, I've already got a nosy neighbor," he murmured, his breath ruffling her hair—and her nerves. "So, on Saturday we're going to get ourselves one big, goofy dog."

The following Saturday afternoon, Patrick pointed his truck out of town, trying his best not to stare at the woman seated next to him.

It wasn't easy.

Torey had shown up wearing faded jeans and a

red sweater, her dark hair loose around her face. When she'd walked toward him, smiling in the afternoon sunlight, Patrick had felt the jolt of it all the way to his boots.

It felt strange, having her sitting beside him in his truck again, traveling familiar roads—roads they'd driven down plenty of times together and which hadn't changed much. Add in the sound of kids' voices coming from the truck's back seat, and it was like all his old daydreams had come true. It was…sweet and painful at the same time and made his heart feel like he'd dragged it over gravel.

"Patrick?"

Torey was looking at him quizzically. Had she said something?

"Sorry. What?"

"Is it far to the—where we're going?"

The dog was a surprise, so ever since Torey had arrived, they'd been speaking in a secret short-hand. Another reminder of high school, when they'd had plenty of code words and private jokes.

"Only about ten more minutes." He glanced in the rearview. Josh was staring out the window, trying to look bored but not quite managing it. Jill was bouncing up and down in her seat.

It was a perfect day for this expedition. Fall had arrived, blown in by a cold front. The air was pleasantly crisp, and the trees on the mountains were shifting from their summer green to gold, red and orange.

When he nosed the truck onto a winding gravel road, he got another sideways look from Torey.

"We're going up Big Pig?"

"Yep." Big Pig was the nickname the locals had given this particular mountain. It was steep and sparsely dotted with shabby cabins, perched on whatever bit of level ground the builders could scrape from the hillside.

"Big Pig's a funny name." Jill's voice piped from the back. "Why do they call it that?"

"Nobody knows for sure, Jillybean. I've heard there used to be wild hogs running through these hills years ago. Maybe an extra big one lived on this mountain."

"A wild piggie lives here?" Jilly clapped her hands. "I hope we see him!"

Torey and Patrick exchanged a glance. "Not likely," Patrick said. "That was a long time ago. Anyway, wild hogs aren't very…uh…cute."

Nothing about this mountain was cute. The poorly maintained road meandered past cabins in various stages of collapse. Many looked abandoned, and the ones that were still occupied didn't look much better.

"Um. Not trying to second-guess you, but are you sure about this?" Torey murmured.

He knew what she meant. A dog that came

from Big Pig might not be the kind of dog he wanted.

"It's okay. This guy's a friend of mine. Sort of." More importantly, the description of the mixed breed female dog had sounded exactly like what he was looking for. Even-tempered and past the puppy stage. Already spayed and safe with kids. Housebroken and medium-sized. This dog had ticked all the right boxes.

He'd been thinking about getting a dog for a while. And, according to the articles he'd read, animals could sometimes reach kids when nobody else could.

He'd figured it was worth a try.

Still. The farther they got up the mountain, the less sure he felt. He hadn't seen Ed Jenkins in a long time, and the man was crusty on a good day.

Well, too late to turn back now.

Ed's cabin was about three-quarters of the way up Big Pig. Patrick turned off the road at a battered metal mailbox, following a rutted driveway.

"Where are we going?" Josh demanded from the back seat, sounding concerned. It was the first thing he'd said since getting in the truck.

"You'll see." Patrick spoke cheerfully, but he was getting an uneasy feeling about this himself. He hadn't been up to Ed's place in years. The driveway was narrower than he remembered, hemmed in by trees and underbrush. On the right-hand side, it sloped downward at a steep angle.

Finally, he drove into a clearing with a small unpainted cabin, weathered gray, and an even smaller barn, just big enough for the '58 Chevy he could see through the door.

Ed's place was the same as he remembered—as plain and harsh as the old mechanic himself. For years, Jenkins Garage had been the rival of R.C.'s Hometown Garage and Ed had come out on the losing side. Both men were good mechanics, but Ron Callahan was as charming as Ed was prickly, and that made a difference in a small town. Still, although the men hadn't been friends, they'd respected each other's abilities. When Ed had broken his right arm and couldn't work for a while, Ron had sent Patrick to help him out for a few weeks.

It had seemed like a generous gesture, but it had actually been a bribe—one that had backfired in a way Ron Callahan could never have foreseen.

"Wait in the truck." Patrick opened the door and got out. The air was chilly and smelled of woodsmoke. Wisps of smoke curled from the cabin's stone chimney, likely from an earlier fire that had since been allowed to go out. Up here, the autumn mornings got pretty brisk.

He made it four steps toward the cabin when the front door opened. Ed stepped outside wearing a plaid shirt and a pair of khaki work pants that had seen better days.

Ed looked like he'd seen better days, too. He must be... What, now? In his late seventies, anyway, but he looked older.

"Patrick."

"Ed." Patrick mounted the steps and held out his hand. "Good to see you."

"Been a while. I don't get down to town so much these days." The man accepted the handshake, his grip surprisingly strong. Patrick got ready for the question he knew was coming. "Still keeping your nose clean and your hands dirty?"

"Yep."

The faded blue eyes gave him a once-over, and Ed seemed satisfied with what he saw. "Fair enough. So, you're here about this dog I been looking after?"

"That's right." When Patrick had heard Ed was fostering shelter dogs until they were adopted, he'd been surprised—for a minute. Then it had made sense. It was the sort of thing Ed would do. Ed didn't put up with nonsense, but he had a kinder heart than most people knew.

"Animal shelter lady said you'd filled out all the forms, and she felt like you'd do good enough. Wanted to know what I thought. I told her in my experience, you was trustworthy."

Patrick swallowed. *Trustworthy.* That's what Ed had called him that day in his garage.

*You seem like a trustworthy boy. I've been watching. Testing you some. Left money out and such. You didn't touch it, and you're a fine worker. So, how come you're helping your daddy and your no-good relatives steal?*

Patrick had felt like he'd been punched. He hadn't known—until that moment—what his father and cousins were doing. Ed had made it all clear. Then he'd given Patrick a choice.

*I told your daddy I was goin' to the police if he didn't come clean himself. But Ron's weak. All he did was tell his nephews, and they took it on themselves to try to make a point.* Ed had gestured to his cast. *Your dad feels bad, so he sent you here so my garage wouldn't go under. But I don't take to threats nor bribes. I respect honesty, though, so I'll make you the same deal I made your daddy. You go to the police yourself, and I mean today, and maybe you can cut yourself and your daddy a deal. Otherwise, I'm telling them everything I know, and son, I know plenty.*

Patrick cleared his throat. "I appreciate that, Ed."

"Hold your horses." Ed raised one bushy eyebrow. "You're good enough for us. Whether or not you're good enough for Dog remains to be seen. She's inside. I'll bring her on out to the porch. You get them young 'uns out of the car, and we'll see how everybody gets along."

Without another word, the man disappeared into the cabin, shutting the battered wooden door behind himself. Torey rolled down the truck window.

"Everything okay?"

"So far so good. Come on out." The kids opened their doors, looking around uncertainly. "There's somebody I'd like you to meet.

Josh circled the truck to stand by Jill. "That old man?"

"Not exactly. We're here to meet a dog."

"A doggie?" Jill squealed, clapping her hands. "Is he coming home with us?"

Even Josh looked interested.

"She. It's a girl. And yeah, that's the idea if things work out," Patrick said cautiously. "We'll know once we meet her."

The door opened, and Ed stepped onto the porch. "Come on," he coaxed. "Nobody's gonna hurt you, not with old Ed standing by."

A trembling young dog stepped outside. She was multicolored—black, brown, and white, her coat slightly shaggy. She had small triangular ears that perked up with interest when she noticed Josh and Jill. Her tail wagged slowly, but then she glanced up at Patrick, her brown eyes worried.

"Men spook her," Ed explained. "She gets over it, but to start with she's real skittish. Been mistreated. Loves kids, though. If you'll step aside and get out of the way, she'll likely go straight to your boy and girl there."

Your boy and girl. Patrick's heart warmed. Cedar Ridge was a small town. If he'd heard about Ed fostering dogs, likely Ed had heard about Patrick's situation, too. That choice of words was no accident.

As soon as Patrick had moved a safe distance away, the dog bolted off the porch, dancing around the kids happily. Jill dropped to her knees and held out her arms, and the dog licked her face while the little girl giggled.

Jill was a sucker for any kind of animal. They'd already hosted the kindergarten class gerbil three times.

Patrick was more worried about her brother's reaction. Josh was watching the dog with cautious interest. Patrick sent up a hopeful prayer.

This dog was his secret weapon. He wasn't sure if anything could convince Josh there was a world beyond his computer screens, but a dog... A dog might just do the trick.

The dog finished washing Jill's face and turned to sniff Josh, her tail slowing to a more cautious speed. The boy reached out a hand, and the dog flinched.

"Go slow, Josh," Torey murmured. "Hold your hand out and tuck your fingers underneath your palm. Let her smell you before you try to pet her."

"Your girlfriend knows a thing or two about dogs," Ed muttered.

Patrick opened his mouth to correct him, then stopped short. It didn't matter that Ed was mistaken about their relationship.

Josh followed Torey's instructions. The dog

sniffed his hand, her tail wagging harder. Finally, Josh petted her head, and the dog plopped her rear on the ground, staring up at him adoringly.

"Well," Ed said. "Looks like you folks have got yourselves a dog."

"Hey, Mr.—" Jill considered him with an uncertain expression. "Mr. Man," she went on finally. "What's the doggie's name?"

"I just been calling her Dog," Ed said. "Seeing as how she was only here temporary-like. Don't know what the folks who had her before called her. Don't care, neither."

"Why not?" Jill asked.

"Because they were mean to her." Josh stroked the dog's head as her tail swept the fallen leaves left and right on the ground. "Whatever name they gave her, it ain't her name anymore. We'll give her a new name." He looked fiercely at his little sister. "I'll name her," he said. "I want to. But...not right now. I need to think about it."

"The shelter lady left papers for you to sign," Ed said gruffly. "And I got some dog food to hold you over until you can get to the store."

"Thanks," Patrick said.

"Yes," Torey added. "It's a really nice thing you're doing, fostering animals."

The older man shrugged. "Don't thank me. I don't do it for the people. I do it for the animals. But," he added, his gaze lingering on Josh, "I admit, it does give me some pleasure to see a dog matched up with the right folks. She'll be happy with those young 'uns. That's all that matters to me."

The dog was happy with Josh and Jill. Torey was allowed to stroke her head, too. But anytime Patrick came near, she scurried away, showing the whites of her eyes.

The papers were signed in short order, making the dog officially theirs. Josh had little trouble enticing her into the truck, although when Patrick got in, she panicked, whimpering and cowering in the back seat. She pressed close to Josh, burying her head in his lap.

"You're okay," the boy assured her. "I'll take good care of you."

"*We'll* take good care of her," Jill protested. "She's not only your dog."

"Don't you worry, little missy," Ed said. "That dog's heart is big enough for both of you." He nodded to Patrick. "Good to see you."

"Likewise, Ed."

Ed stepped back and walked back toward the cabin.

"Let me out!"

Patrick glanced into the rearview and saw Jill fumbling with the door handle. "Whoa, Jillybean!" he protested. "Best not open that door. The dog's liable to run off. She's not used to us yet."

"But I need to hug Mr. Man." Jill continued trying the door handle with an uncharacteristic stubbornness. "He's sad 'cause the doggie's leaving."

Patrick looked at Ed's plaid-covered back. "Oh, I don't think so, sweetie. He knew the dog would only live here until she found her forever home."

"But he loved her anyhow! Just like you love me and Josh. Won't you be lonesome, Paddy? When me and Josh go away? I will. I'm going to cry and cry and cry. Mr. Man's being brave, but I think he might cry, too, and I want to hug his neck!"

She sounded near tears herself, and Patrick's heart turned to mush.

"Let her." Torey's dark eyes sparkled suspiciously—Torey, who never cried.

"Hold on to that dog, Josh," Patrick said. Then he disabled the child locks.

Jill dashed across the yard to Ed, who was almost to his steps. He paused, then leaned down to accept a very enthusiastic hug.

Patrick caught sight of Ed's face as Jill's arms went around his neck, and then the scene went blurry.

Jill was right. The old guy did look sad. That wasn't the only thing the little girl was right about, either.

"Patrick." Torey was watching him.

She didn't say another word, but, just like the old days, she didn't need to. He knew what she was thinking. He was thinking the same thing.

He wasn't just going to ask Mitzi about adopting Josh and Jill. He was going to push for it, for Jill's sake—and for Josh's.

And for his.

"I know," he said, not daring to say too much since Josh was in the back seat.

Torey nodded at him—one short, firm nod. "You can do this."

"I'm not so sure." But as he watched Ed leading Jill back to the truck, his face wreathed in a rusty smile, Patrick knew he had to try.

"I am," Torey retorted. "And if I can help, let me know."

Their eyes met. Her cheeks went pink, and her gaze skittered off.

"Thanks," he said as Jill climbed into the truck. Ed shut the door carefully behind her. "I'll hold you to that."

# Chapter Seven

"I'm leaving, Ruby," Torey slung her purse over her shoulder and drained the last of her coffee. "Do you need anything before I head to Jorgeson's?"

"Not a thing." Ruby took the mug from her hand, plopping it into the sudsy dishwater. "My," she added. "Look at you. Mighty fancy clothes for wandering around a pumpkin farm."

Torey glanced down at her skirt and yellow blouse and felt a flicker of doubt. "The skirt's denim, and I'm wearing boots. I think it'll be fine." It would, she told herself. It had taken her an embarrassingly long time to choose this outfit, and she couldn't waste time picking out another one. "We're taking pictures of the farm to put on the Hope Center's social media. I figured I'd better look nice."

"Mmm." Ruby pursed her lips and lifted up a glass of orange juice. She peered at it, carefully wiping away a spot. "You want to look nice for the *pictures*."

"That's right." The outfit she'd picked had nothing to do with the fact that she'd be seeing Patrick today.

Ruby gave the dishcloth a fierce twist. "I thought Patrick was going to handle these activities by himself while you managed other things at the center."

Torey frowned at her. "Ruby, is there some reason you don't want me to go? Do you need me to stay here with you today?"

"No!" Ruby protested quickly. "I just figured one of you'd need to be at the center with the kids who didn't want to go to the farm today."

"We decided to close for the day. It's simpler just to have one activity option open at a time. And it's just one afternoon. The Hope Center will be open tomorrow as usual." Torey paused, puzzled. That sort of comment was so unlike Ruby. "The Jorgesons are doing most of the supervising, so Patrick could have handled today alone, but the lady who brought me up taught me to do my fair share of a job."

Ruby didn't crack a smile. "I thought your job was getting those computers set up. And that's done, ain't it?"

Torey crossed her arms, studying the older woman. This was confusing. She'd have expected Ruby to be ecstatic at the prospect of Torey and an eligible man spending an afternoon together at the picturesque Jorgensen farm. Surely that ticked all sorts of matchmaking boxes. "Ruby, are you sure you're all right? Maybe I should stay here after all."

"Don't be silly. Ain't nothing wrong with me, and Charlotte's coming by to help me with some sewing, so I won't be by myself."

"Good." Torey nodded, relieved. "Tell her that fabric she ordered for the costumes came in, so she's all set to start that class next week." Charlotte had enthusiastically agreed to help the children design and sew their costumes for the Harvest Parade, and the sewing class had been officially added to the center's schedule.

"I'll let her know. And while we're on the subject, I might as well let you know something else. I'm going to help her."

"Ruby—" Torey began, alarmed.

"I'll take it easy, and I can sew sitting down. Y'all can babysit me just as well there, and at least I'll be making myself useful. I got to start getting into the swing of things. You'll need to go back to Atlanta soon."

"Not for a while yet, so don't worry about that." Torey looked her mom over for another minute. She seemed fine. There was a nice flush of color in her cheeks and a brisk efficiency to her movements. "Okay," Torey conceded. "The Hope Center can certainly use the help so long as you don't tire yourself out."

"Good. That's all settled. Now get on with you. You don't want to keep Patrick waiting." She snorted and rinsed another orange juice glass. "He might end up having to manage on his own, and you wouldn't want that, now, would you?"

"Ruby," Torey started, but the older woman waved her away with an impatient hand.

"Don't mind me. Go on now. Get!"

As Torey drove down the mountain, she replayed the conversation in her head. Ruby had been behaving oddly lately when the topics of Patrick or the Hope Center came up. And not oddly in the way Torey had expected. She wasn't pushing Patrick at her at all. In fact, she seemed to be doing the opposite.

Other than that, though, Ruby was getting back to normal, and she'd had a good report from her doctor yesterday. Torey made a mental note to discuss this Patrick-related oddity with her siblings and put it out of her mind.

She had a pleasant day ahead of her, and she planned to enjoy it.

She could have stayed at the center today and worked. There was always plenty to do. But she'd really enjoyed the trip with Patrick and the kids up to Big Pig last weekend. The ride back down the mountain had been chaotic and fun.

The dog wasn't accustomed to car rides, and she'd whimpered. Josh had comforted her in a low, steady voice.

"You're all right. Nobody's going to hurt you no more."

There was a certain determined tone in the boy's voice that had sent a tickle up Torey's spine. It could have been Patrick himself talking.

She'd darted a glance at him. He'd been frowning through the windshield, carefully navigating their way on the rutted road leading down Big Pig. Colorful autumn branches brushed past the truck as the overhanging trees crowded close, leaving yellow and red leaves sprinkled over the truck like confetti.

He'd caught her looking, and half his mouth had tipped up in a smile. "Don't worry. This road is rough, but the truck can handle it. I'll get us to the bottom of the mountain in one piece."

She couldn't help it. He'd sounded so much like Josh that she'd started to laugh—but somehow the sound got tangled up in her throat.

"I know you will," she'd managed finally.

She did know it, and so did the kids. They were happily focused on the dog, trusting Patrick to get them safely home. For ordinary kids, it wouldn't be so unusual, but for foster kids to trust like that… Torey understood better than most how huge that was.

She wasn't surprised, though. There was something about Patrick—a quiet, solid reliability— that made a person feel safe around him. She'd felt that way, too, once. And when he'd broken up with her, she'd felt so…vulnerable and hurt. He'd promised to love her and then ditched her, just like her bio mom had. Her heart still ached at the memory, even now, all these years later.

She blinked and came to her senses. She'd reached the end of Ruby's driveway. As she turned onto the road, she also deliberately turned her mind away from her past with Patrick and back to the whole point of today—bolstering the Hope Center.

Attendance at the center was picking up nicely. More kids were stopping by in the afternoons, and the computer lab was a big draw. But not the only one. Patrick's two classes were also full, and he'd had to start a waiting list for his next ones. The art class was so productive that the halls of the old Victorian had been transformed into an amateur art gallery, and the teacher was canvassing local stores for donations of supplies.

The budget remained a problem, and the Center's newfound popularity had caused some others. There'd been a few scuffles, some items had gone missing, and others had been damaged. Some of the children seemed allergic to following any sort of rules or directions, and Barton Myers missed no opportunity to complain. But the high school counselor and the local ministers Patrick had drafted were counseling the kids with recurrent behavioral problems, and overall, Torey thought things were going well.

She'd found a lot of satisfaction in solving the problems that cropped up. Too much satisfaction maybe. Her mind flicked to what Ruby had said about Atlanta.

Torey's boss would be delighted to have her cut her leave short. It might even get her back into Cal's good graces. And Ruby and the center were both doing well.

She could go back anytime. But she didn't want to cut her time in Cedar Ridge short. In spite of all the hard work and long hours, she felt like a kid at an amusement park, and she didn't want to miss a moment of the fun.

Speaking of that, maybe she'd better swing by the center and see if any stragglers needed a ride to the Jorgeson's farm. The Jorgesons had been excited about the Hope Center's field trip, and they'd generously offered to provide transportation as well as supervision. If the kids filled out permission slips, they'd be picked up by the farm van at school.

But Torey had learned that the children—and their parents—weren't reliable about following directions. Some might have shown up at the Center, even though everybody had been notified it would be closed this afternoon.

She didn't want anybody left there unsupervised, so she'd make a quick detour. And if somebody had shown up, she could give them a ride to the farm.

When she pulled up to the old Victorian, she saw no children milling around—that was good. But a man stood on the porch, his back to her, peering through the glass and knocking on the door.

Probably Barton Myers, Torey thought irritably. The man lived close enough to walk to the center, and he'd been a frequent and unwelcome visitor. He was causing all the problems he could—making noise complaints, questioning zoning regulations, writing letters to the editor of the newspaper demanding the center be closed permanently.

She considered driving past without stopping. But then she groaned, put on her blinker, and turned into the driveway. Barton was persistent, and when he couldn't get in touch with her or with Patrick, he pestered Ruby. She couldn't allow that.

As she walked toward the porch, the man turned, and she stopped short.

"Ron?"

Patrick's father grinned. "Well, if it ain't Torey-my-glory! Long time no see, sweetheart." He chuckled self-consciously. "'Course the places I been, I wouldn't have wanted to see you. But it's sure good to see you now."

Torey didn't know what to say. She'd been psyched up to battle Barton Myers, not deal with a man she hadn't laid eyes on in over ten years.

She'd not seen Ron Callahan since he went to prison.

Ron was a talker, so he went on without much encouragement. "I'm looking for Patrick. I stopped by his garage, but it was closed. I asked around, and folks said he's spending most afternoons here, helping out at the Hope Center." Ron paused. "With you." There was a question in his voice.

"We're just stepping in to run it until they find a permanent director," she said shortly.

"Said he was teaching classes out here. That so?"

"It is. He's good at it, too."

An incredulous smile broke over Ron's face. "Ain't that something? That boy always could do just about anything he put his mind to. You reckon he'll be along anytime soon? I don't mind waiting."

Torey hesitated. "Not today," she said finally. "We have a field trip for the kids over at Jorgeson's farm."

"Oh." Ron's face fell. "That's a shame. I'm a little short on gas money, so I hitched a ride out here, hoping to see him." The older man scratched at his graying hair. "He's been a hard fella to get hold of. Seems like he's mighty busy these days."

"Yes, I guess he is."

She didn't know what relationship Patrick and Ron had now. Patrick hadn't mentioned his fa-

ther, and she'd assumed that Ron was still out of
his life.

But maybe not. In any case, she'd always liked
Ron, in spite of his faults. And he'd never been
anything but kind to her. "I have to get out to the
farm myself," she said. "But I can give you a ride
someplace first, if you want."

Ron's face lit up. "That's kind of you, but I
don't want to take you out of your way."

"Oh, that's no troub—" Torey started, but Ron
butted in.

"So you can just drive me on out to Jorgeson's.
I mean, since you're going that way anyhow." He
beamed at her. "That'll solve both our problems,
won't it? And it'll give us a real good chance to
catch up."

Torey decided to go with honesty. "No offense,
Ron, but are you sure Patrick's going to be happy
to see you?"

Ron's eyebrows went up. "You always were a
straight shooter, Torey. No, honey, I'm not sure of
that at all. Truth is, the boy's been dodging me."

"Then you'd better not go to Jorgeson's." This
was absolutely none of her business, not anymore.
But the words came out anyway. "You hurt him,
Ron. You lied to him, and you made him a part
of something illegal. You knew how he felt about
that. He asked you to turn yourself in, and you
wouldn't do it, so he had to. I'm not saying you
don't deserve a second chance, but—"

"He gave me a second chance, Torey. I blew that one, too. Stole something from him because I was low on cash and in a tight spot with the family."

"Ron." Torey didn't even know what to say to that.

"I'm not denying the wrong I did. I want to tell him I'm sorry to his face. And I am sorry, Torey, and I've changed, I really have. I haven't been in trouble for a long time. I just don't know how to get him to believe it. He won't even talk to me."

Torey bit down on her lower lip. Sincerity and regret rang in Ron's voice, and oh, could she relate. She'd been frozen out by Patrick, too, and she remembered how desperate she'd felt. If he'd just talk to her, just let her explain...

"I'm sorry," she said. "But I can't help you, and if I can't give you a ride someplace else, I need to get going."

Ron's face fell, but he nodded. "That's okay. You go ahead and don't worry about me. But Torey, if you've still got a soft spot left in your heart for a lonesome old man, you might say a word in Patrick's ear for me. Tell him what I've told you. He won't listen to me, but he might listen to you."

Torey sighed. "I wouldn't count on that."


"Want me to go in the corn maze with you?" Patrick asked casually, not sure what the protocol here was. Would they want him with them? Or not?

Parenting, he'd discovered, was full of this kind of stuff. He sometimes felt like he was trying to rebuild an engine blindfolded.

"Nah," Josh said. "None of the other kids got grown-ups with them. We want to figure it out by ourselves."

"You'll keep track of Jill?"

Josh shot him a look. "I always do."

"That's true," Patrick said. "You do. Well…" He grabbed a tall pole with a white flag attached and handed it to Josh. "If you get stumped, wave this. The guy in the tower will see you, and—"

"I don't need that." Josh puffed out his small chest. "We ain't gonna get lost."

"Take it just in case." Patrick wiggled the pole. "Unless you'd rather I go with you."

"Okay," Josh groaned. "But you worry too much." He kicked at a pebble on the ground. "You sure we can't take Lexie with us?"

Lexie was the name Josh had settled on for the dog. He hadn't offered any particular explanation for his choice, and Patrick hadn't pushed it. He could name the dog whatever he wanted.

"I'm sorry, but no, you can't. The Jorgesons have a rule that dogs can't go in the maze. Even on leashes. Don't worry. Lexie and I will be right here waiting for you when you come out, and we'll go get snacks from the food truck."

"Will Miss Torey be here, too?" Jill piped up hopefully. She and Josh had loved going to Big

Pig with Torey. "She could eat snacks with us, maybe."

"Sure, if she wants to."

Josh knelt on the ground. The boy put his arms around Lexie, burying his face in her neck. He murmured to her, as the dog licked his ear. Then the boy got back to his feet, gave Patrick a sideways, half-embarrassed look and reached for his sister's hand.

"Take good care of Lexie," Josh ordered. "That collar still don't fit her right, even after we put the new holes in it. And she ain't gonna like me being gone."

"She won't, but we'll manage." Patrick winked. "Maybe I'm not the only one who worries too much."

Josh snorted, but he gave the dog a long, last look as he led his sister into the maze.

"Have fun!" Patrick called after them.

As they disappeared into the stalks, Lexie whined and strained at her leash. Patrick chuckled. "I know how you feel, girl, but you and I have to wait this out."

He looked around at the happy confusion. Jorgeson's had welcomed the Hope Center kids with open arms, offering complimentary snacks and free admission to the extra activities like the corn maze and the petting zoo.

He wandered over to the animal area and smiled at the younger kids petting a selection of amiable llamas, goats, and miniature donkeys. Jina, Torey's younger sister, was supervising. He'd heard she lived in Rockmart now, and that she was an elementary school teacher, so she must have driven over for the day to help out. She was wearing a Volunteer button shaped like a pumpkin—and quietly feeding the food pellet dispenser with quarters from her own pocket, then passing the feed to the kids.

He approached, fishing out a handful of change. "Let me help with that."

Jina's warm smile faded when she recognized him. "Not necessary. Today is our treat."

Patrick shoved the change back into his pocket, feeling embarrassed. "It's really nice what the Jorgesons are doing," he said. "We appreciate it." Especially since he knew the little farm had some financial troubles.

"Anything for the kids. Watch your dog," she added sharply.

Patrick looked down. Lexie was straining at the end of her leash, attempting to get under the fence into the llama enclosure.

"Sorry." He picked the dog up. "We just adopted her, so she's still learning. We probably shouldn't have brought her, but my foster son's already very attached to her, and the website said dogs were welcome."

"They are. Just keep her out of the animal areas, please, and away from their food and water. That's farm policy because it protects our livestock from diseases and injuries. Now, if you don't mind, I need to get back to work." She turned her back and walked away, prompting a concerned look from a guy helping oversee the petting zoo area.

"Who's that?" he murmured, giving Patrick a suspicious once-over.

"Nobody important," Jina responded, making sure her voice was loud enough for Patrick to overhear. She patted the young man's arm, a small engagement ring twinkling. Her fiancé smiled at her. But when she bent to help a Hope Center child feed pellets to a llama, he sent Patrick a better-back-off look.

Patrick didn't want trouble, so he left, walking past the food trucks and toward the exit of the corn maze. The afternoon was still as bright and the kids just as happy, but some of the gloss was gone, at least for him.

He'd always liked Jina, and it bugged him to get the cold shoulder from her. But he understood. Torey's family was ferociously loyal to each other. He'd hurt Torey, and Jina wouldn't forget that easily.

None of them would. He'd gotten similar reactions from the rest of Torey's siblings when he'd bumped into them over the years, even Sheriff Logan Carter, who'd once been his best friend. Only Ruby had forgiven him—or so he'd thought.

Now he wondered. Maybe the whole "get Torey to go back to Atlanta" thing was in part because Ruby wanted to put some distance between them.

He couldn't put his finger on why, exactly, this was bothering him so much now. Maybe spending time with Torey again was raking up his regrets about how things had ended between them.

"Here." He looked up. Jina stood beside him, a plastic bowl of water in one hand. "For your dog."

"Thanks." He stooped to place it on the ground. Lexie lapped up the water gratefully.

"You'd better get her a harness if you're going to put her on a leash. She's likely to slip that collar."

"We'll make a stop at the pet store on the way home." He paused. "Thanks for the advice. And congratulations on your engagement. He looks like a good guy."

"He is." Jina hesitated, looking both irritated and uncomfortable. "Look," she said. "I'm sorry if I was rude before. I just... I always liked you, Patrick. We all did. But after what happened..."

"I know."

"Do you?" A hint of steel came into Jina's soft voice. "Do you know that I've only seen my sister cry twice? Only twice in all these years. Once when she turned eighteen, and Ruby told her she didn't have to leave, no matter what the foster care system said. That she had a family forever, no matter what."

Patrick swallowed. "I remember that day."

"Want to guess what the second time was?" When he didn't answer, she went on. "Ruby told me you're a foster dad, and I've been watching you with those two kids. Since I was in the system myself, I'm pretty good at telling the good parents from the rotten ones. You're one of the good ones."

"Thanks, Jina."

"That's the only reason I'm talking to you right now. Well. Actually, there's one other reason. And she's walking this way."

Patrick looked over to see Torey heading toward them. She was framed by low-hanging branches heavy with colorful leaves, the sun brightening her yellow shirt and finding hidden highlights in her dark hair. She waved, and his breath caught in his throat.

She was beautiful.

"Patrick?" Jina frowned at him. "I don't know what's going on with you and Torey. I mean, I know you're working together, but the way you're looking at her seems pretty personal to me. I'd appreciate it—we'd all appreciate it—if you thought this through very carefully before you say or do anything you can't take back. Torey might not wear her feelings on her sleeve, but that doesn't mean she doesn't have them. If you make my sister cry again…" Jina shook her head. "Just don't," she finished.

She moved away from him toward Torey, whom she greeted with a hug. The sound of sisterly laughter drifted to him, and a pang of envy hit when he saw Torey's expression—so warm and open and unguarded.

She used to look at him that way.

After another quick hug, Jina departed, and Torey resumed walking in his direction, the smile lingering on her lips.

"Hi!" She leaned to ruffle Lexie's ears. "Sorry I'm late. How are things going so far?" She shaded her eyes with one hand, scanning the busy farm. "Looks like a roaring success."

"The kids seem to be having a good time."

"Speaking of kids, where are Josh and Jill?"

"In the corn maze. I wasn't allowed to go with them. Apparently having a parent along ruins the fun."

Torey laughed, and his heart jumped. "Having you along definitely would."

"Thanks."

Torey slapped his arm lightly. "Oh, you know what I mean. With your sense of direction, you'd be out of that thing in thirty seconds flat. You couldn't get lost if you tried."

"I don't know about that." Patrick wasn't even sure what he was saying. He was too busy noticing the way Torey's eyes sparkled when she was teasing. "I've felt pretty lost a time or two. And

I've definitely ended up in some places I never meant to go."

Maybe it was his tone that caught Torey's attention. She looked at him, a faint line creasing her forehead. "Well, that happens to the best of us, but Ruby always says a detour doesn't have to be a destination. If you get where you're meant to be in the end, that's all that matters."

"Did you? Get where you're meant to be?" He didn't know why he was asking that question, only that he wanted to know the answer.

She hesitated. "In the one way that really matters, I did."

"What does that mean?"

Her cheeks flushed. "I'm not much good at talking about it, but it took me a while to make my peace with God. For a long time, I didn't care what He said about right and wrong. I just did whatever it took to look after myself and the people who mattered to me."

He remembered that Torey. The most loyal person he'd ever met, but with a recklessness that had knocked the breath out of him more than once.

"You're here taking care of Ruby, so I'd say you're still pretty determined to look after the people who matter to you."

"True," Torey admitted. "I just try to…respect the rules a little better now." She gave him a quizzical smile. "Why are we playing twenty questions?"

"I don't know." He didn't. None of this was

any of his business anymore. "Probably because it distracts me from worrying about the kids. I thought they'd be back by now. Silly, I know. They're in a corn maze having the time of their lives." Lexie had lost interest in her water, so he dumped the remainder out and set the bowl on a nearby hay bale where Jina could easily find it.

"You're right. It's silly." When he cut her a sideways look, she laughed and went on. "In a good way, though. Every kid needs to have somebody willing to worry about them. When I came to Ruby's, I acted like it bothered me, her wanting to know where I was and what I was doing all the time. Fussing over me when I had a cold, making sure I did my homework, stuff like that." She paused. "But the truth is, it felt…safe, knowing that an adult cared." She lifted her chin. "If I hadn't had that, I don't think I'd ever have been able to believe that God cared. You'll get through to Josh, too, if you keep at it."

"I'm going to."

They looked at each other, and Torey offered him a smile—a polite, friendly smile. There was no reason for his heart to decide to do a drum solo, but it did anyway.

"I'm going over to the corn maze exit to wait for the kids." He hesitated. "We were planning to grab some snacks afterward. Want to come with?"

A slight, almost undetectable pause. "Sure."

They started toward the end of the maze, Lexie straining at the end of her leash, her tail wagging furiously. Patrick shook his head.

"It's like Lexie knows we're going to find Josh."

"Lexie?"

"According to Josh, that's her name."

"It suits her. So, the whole dog idea is working out for you?"

"It is. Jill loves her, too, but Josh has really bonded with her. It's early days, but so far he hasn't balked about walking her and cleaning up after her. He lets Jill make sure her water bowl is full, but only because she begged him to let her help. And I caught him secretly pouring it out, scrubbing it and refilling it when she wasn't looking." Patrick drew in a deep breath of autumn air, richly scented with apples, pumpkins, animals, and the dusty smell of cornstalks. "He still loves his screens too much, but the dog's definitely helping."

"That's good."

There was an odd note in her voice. Patrick started to ask her about it, but they'd reached the exit area of the corn maze. He did a hopeful recon, but he didn't see either of the kids. Lexie sniffed hard, and her tail wagging speed increased. She tugged at the leash and whined urgently.

"They must not be too far off," he said. "I think Lexie smells them."

"Probably." There it was again. That strange, uptight note in her voice.

He sighed. "What is it?" When she just looked at him, he went on. "You want to say something, but you're holding back. You might as well go ahead and spit it out."

"All right." She paused. "It's just that Josh isn't your average computer-obsessed kid, Patrick. Like I told you, he's got serious skills. My computer geek friends were amazed that he managed to get past all their safeguards and access that game."

"That's nothing to brag about."

Torey's eyes flashed. "Well, it is, and it isn't, Patrick. He shouldn't have sidestepped the rules. That's a given. But the fact that he was able to do it, and at his age…believe me, that's impressive."

"And?" Patrick tugged Lexie gently back. Josh must be getting closer because the dog was growing increasingly frantic.

"And that level of ability puts Josh in a different category, that's all. I'm not saying he shouldn't have other interests, but he's like a… I don't know…a computer prodigy."

"A prodigy? You mean like you were?" Lexie was gnawing on her leash. "No, no!" Patrick leaned over to extract the thick vinyl strap from the dog's mouth. Lexie instantly cowered down on the ground, trembling, rolling her eyes up at him. "It's okay," he murmured, stroking the dog's head. She'd been doing much better with him, but any quick moves upset her.

"Josh is much higher level than I was at his age." The firmness in her voice got his attention. He got to his feet. He wasn't comforting the dog, anyhow—only Josh could do that.

"What does that mean, exactly?"

"It means he's unusually gifted."

"I know what prodigy means, Torey. I mean what does it mean if Josh is one?"

"There's not really an *if* here. And a kid with these skills, it's like…" Torey seemed to be searching for words. "It's like handing a toddler a power drill. He's going to need some expert guidance, or—"

"Or he'll end up getting himself into some real trouble." Frustration and worry made Patrick's tone sharp. How exactly was he going to handle this? He didn't know beans about computers.

"Right. Just like I did."

"Torey, I didn't mean—"

That was as far as he got. The leash in his hand went slack, and he looked down just in time to see Lexie bounding through the cornstalks into the maze, barking her head off.

"Lexie!" Cornstalks waved furiously in the wake of the disappearing dog. Patrick started into the maze, threading his way past triumphant kids on their way out.

Torey was right behind him. "It'll be okay. She'll find Josh and stick with him." They rounded a bend and stopped, confronted with three possible paths. "Whether we can find them or not is the question."

"That way," Patrick said grimly, pointing to cornstalks wiggling in the distance.

"Well, yeah, but how do we get there?"

"The maze is cut in the shape of a pig. We're at the snout end, and I think they're at the eye." Patrick did a few calculations. "This way," he decided, choosing the path on the left.

Torey jogged beside him, sidestepping more squealing children. "How did you know about the shape of the maze?"

"There's an aerial photo on their website. We turn here." He took a right.

"What did you do, memorize it?"

Well, yeah. "I wanted to be sure I could go in after any kids who couldn't find their way out."

"Don't the Jorgesons have somebody to handle that?"

"They do, but these kids are my responsibility." They rounded a corner, and Patrick felt a surge of relief. Josh and Jill were kneeling in the dirt beside Lexie, who was joyfully licking Josh's cheeks.

Josh looked up, his face like a thundercloud. "You let her go!"

"I didn't let her go, she slipped her collar," Patrick held up the evidence, dangling at the end of the lead.

"She could have gotten hurt. You were supposed to take care of her."

"Hi, guys!" A grandmotherly woman wearing a volunteer badge came up the path. "Sorry, but dogs aren't allowed in the maze. And she'll need to be put back on her leash, please."

"Talk to him," Josh said, glaring at Patrick. "This is his fault." He gathered up the dog in his arms and started down the dusty path.

"Josh," Patrick called after him.

"Leave me alone," the boy said without turning around.

"I'll go with him," Torey murmured. "He probably just needs a minute to calm down. You bring Jill." She hurried after the boy.

"Let your wife handle it," the older woman murmured.

"I'm sorry?"

"Your son, there. Let your wife deal with him right now. Mothers and sons have a special connection." She smiled down at Jill, who was looking up at her, her freckled face smudged and her eyes wide. "Just like daddies and daughters do." She winked at Patrick. "I've raised six kids, three of each, and when they hit the teenaged years, tag teaming really helps. Parenting that age is definitely a two-person job." She unclipped a radio from her belt. "Dog's out of the maze and under control. I'm heading back now." A second later, she'd disappeared through the stalks.

A two-person job. Patrick's mind lingered on the woman's words until he felt a tug on his fingers.

"Can we go, Paddy? I'm hungry."

"Sure thing, Jillybean. Tell you what." He hoisted her onto his shoulders. She squealed with joy—and dug her fingers into his hair, making him wince. "Now you can see. Tell me which way to go."

"That way!" Jill pointed.

Jill proved to be a good navigator, and a minute later they were out of the maze. Josh and Torey were over to the side. Josh was crouched next to the dog, and Torey's hand was on his shoulder.

"It wasn't his fault, Josh." Her clear, calm voice carried to him. "I was standing right there. The collar doesn't fit, and she really wanted to get to you. Nobody could have stopped her."

To his relief, Patrick saw the beginnings of a smile on Josh's face. "Yeah," he muttered. "She really loves me, I think."

"I know she does. And so does Paddy."

Josh looked up at Torey, then, searching her face as if trying to see if she was telling him the truth. Patrick's stomach did a quick flip of gratitude.

He knew Josh admired Torey, and here she was, using that influence to nudge him toward Patrick. That was…

That was really nice of her.

"Paddy, I'm hungry," Jill complained again.

"All right, sweetie. Time for a corn dog. Let's get your brother and head for the food truck."

"But there's a long line."

"I got a corn dog you can have, little lady," a familiar voice said. "Easy enough for me to get another one."

"Thanks, but—" Patrick turned, and found himself face-to-face with the very last person he expected to see. The last person he wanted to see.

"Hi, there, son," Ron Callahan said with a smile.

# Chapter Eight

Torey stiffened. Surely not.

But there was Ron, standing in front of Patrick and Jill. He was holding out a corn dog and looked half hopeful and half embarrassed.

"Come on, Josh," Torey murmured. "Let's go get the leash from your dad."

"My *foster* dad," the boy muttered, but he gathered Lexi up in his arms and followed her.

She closed the space between them fast, her eyes connecting directly with Ron's as she approached. He took a cautious step backward.

"Well, hello, Torey-my-Glory. We meet again."

"What are you doing here, Ron?"

"I was just asking him the same question," Patrick said. Then he frowned. "Again? What does he mean *again*?"

"I bumped into Torey over at that Hope Center place, and she told me y'all were going to be here today. A friend at the filling station loaned me some gas money, so I thought I'd come by, you know, try to catch you so we could have a word."

"Paddy, who's this man?" Jill sounded grumpy, her eyes fixed on the corn dog.

Before Patrick could answer, Ron stepped closer. "Why, I'm Patrick's daddy, that's who. And what's your name, little lady?"

"I'm Jill. And I'm really hungry."

Ron chuckled, and the sound pulled Torey back into the past. How many times had she heard that rich, rolling laugh back when she and Patrick were dating? Plenty. Ron had always been a friendly, easygoing guy.

"Here you go." He handed Jill the corn dog.

Patrick started to protest, but Jill was too quick for him. She took a bite. "Thanks," she mumbled around her mouthful.

Josh studied Ron with narrowed eyes. "This guy's your dad? For real?"

"I sure am. I guess that makes me your honorary grandpa, doesn't it?" He reached out to tousle the boy's hair, but Josh flinched and stepped out of range.

"I need Lexie's collar," he demanded.

Patrick handed it over. "Dad, I'm really busy."

"So you've said. Look, I'm not asking for much, just a few minutes of your time. I'd like to talk to you, explain to you how—"

"How you're different now."

Ron winced, but he nodded. "Pretty much. I'd really appreciate it if you'd hear me out."

"Josh, why don't you and Jill go over to the food truck? Get another corn dog and a couple of drinks, okay?"

Josh hesitated. "What should I do with Lexie?"

"I'll watch her." Patrick reached for the leash, but Josh pulled it out of reach.

"Miss Torey, will you take care of Lexie for me?"

Torey's heart sank as she saw Patrick's expression go a bit grimmer. She was already in trouble, and Josh wasn't helping. "Okay," she said. "Sure, but—"

"I'll be right back. Come on, Jill. Lexie won't be happy without me for long."

Josh led his sister toward the food truck. Lexie whined and pulled on her leash, attempting to follow.

"Lexie, no. Sit," Torey commanded desperately.

The dog whined again, but she plopped her bottom down on the ground.

"Even the dog," Patrick muttered.

"She's got the touch," Ron chuckled. "Now, listen, son. I don't mean to trouble you, and I can see you're busy with the kids. They're real cute, by the way. Let's just set up a time to talk, and I'll get out of your hair so you can go on and enjoy your day."

"I don't—"

"Hi!" Ellen Jorgeson approached at a brisk walk, her snow-white ponytail gleaming in the autumn sunlight. She favored them all with a no-nonsense smile. "Sorry to intrude, but one of our gatekeepers radioed that a gentleman—this gentleman, I'm assuming—talked his way past the gate. The volunteer explained that this was a private event and that the farm was closed to the public, but he said he had an urgent message for Patrick Callahan." She arched an eyebrow. "I'm just checking to make sure everything is all right and to see if the farm can be of any assistance?"

Patrick's gaze slid to his father, who had the grace to look chagrined.

Torey cleared her throat. "He needed to deliver a message, that's all. He's leaving now."

"And everything's all right?" Mrs. Jorgeson inquired coolly.

"Yes. Thank you," Patrick said, not taking his eyes off his father.

"Well, good. Sir, I can escort you to the gate."

"Oh, that won't be necessary," Ron protested.

"Go with her, Dad."

"Oh!" Mrs. Jorgeson's face relaxed. "This is your father. Well, that's perfectly fine, then. Feel free to stay if you'd like."

Ron's face brightened, but Torey shook her head. "Unfortunately, he has to leave now. We appreciate your offer to show him to the gate."

She shot the older man a stern look. "He has some trouble following directions these days."

Mrs. Jorgeson nodded sympathetically. "I see," she said gently. "Come along, sir. It's right this way."

As she led Ron away, he threw one last pleading look over his shoulder. The sadness in the older man's eyes tugged at Torey's heart, but she refused to give in.

"You told my father to come here?" Patrick asked, his face hard.

"I definitely did not. He was looking for you, and I mentioned that we had an event here today, that's all. He asked me for a ride, but I told him I didn't think he should bother you."

Patrick looked skeptical. "Why didn't you mention that when you got here?"

"I don't know. It didn't seem to be a very happy topic, I guess. Then the dog ran away, and everything. Besides, I didn't think it was going to be a problem."

"Well, it is. Or it could be." Patrick's eyes cut over to the kids. They were at the front of the line now, and Josh was accepting two cups from the Jorgeson volunteer. He checked to make sure that the top was on well, and then he handed it to his little sister. "I'm planning to talk to Mitzi and her supervisor about adopting Josh and Jill."

Torey sucked in her breath in a gasp. "That's wonderful, Patrick. That's—"

He shook his head. "Don't get too excited. It's a long shot. I'm already on thin ice because of Josh's behavior. Mitzi thinks I'm not a good foster placement. I can only imagine what she'll think about me adopting them. But if I don't, I'm afraid they'll split them up. They're talking about sending Josh to a group home so they can find a better family for Jill."

Torey couldn't believe what she was hearing—but then again, she could. The foster care system did a lot of good for kids, but it was far from perfect. Heartbreaking situations like this happened all too often. "But you'll keep them together."

"I will if I can convince them to let me. The last thing I need right now is my ex-con of a father hanging around. Mitzi was clear that my family background is a big concern. I just can't risk it."

Torey could understand that. But still. The hurt in Ron's eyes and the doggedness he showed in tracking Patrick down…that counted for something, surely. Her bio mom had never done anything like that.

Torey tried to choose her words carefully. "Ron said something back at the center about how he'd turned his life around. How he hadn't been in trouble for a long time."

"I don't think he has been. At least not as far as I know." When Torey looked at him, Patrick shrugged irritably. "I may not know much about computers, but I know how to use Google."

"Well, if he's really turned his life around, then—" Torey let her question hang in the air unfinished.

Patrick's jaw hardened. "Don't, Torey. Okay? Please. Just don't." Their eyes met, and for a second, it felt as if all those years hadn't passed by at all, as if the hurt between them happened yesterday and was still fresh.

Then he looked away, toward Josh and Jill, who were headed in their direction. "I'm going to sit down and eat a snack with the kids. I'll see you at the center tomorrow afternoon, okay?"

It was a clear dismissal. "Sure. Early, right? I'm bringing Ruby to choose the winner of the float design contest, remember?"

Patrick's expression softened. "That's right. Ruby's going to be there. Good. I'll see you both then."

As he walked away without a backward glance, Torey wondered if he was relieved that they wouldn't be spending any time alone together tomorrow. There'd be no opportunity for uncomfortable conversations.

He probably was. And she should be, too.

She should be. But she wasn't.

The following afternoon, Patrick pulled up to the Hope Center ten minutes late for his meeting with Torey. He sat for a minute in his truck after killing the engine, trying to get his head on straight.

It had been a day.

One thing after another had gone wrong, making his plans fall like a row of dominoes. First, the dog had chewed the corner off Josh's school backpack, effectively destroying it.

"It's not her fault," Josh had protested protectively. "She just don't like me going to school and leaving her."

Then, Jill had cried because he'd forgotten that today was something called "goofy socks day" at her elementary school—and she didn't have any appropriately silly socks to wear. They'd ransacked the house, and she'd finally ended up going to school wearing some of Patrick's socks, a pair printed with purple Edsels, which had been a gift from a client. They were huge on her feet and went all the way up past her knees, and Jill wasn't thrilled about wearing socks with cars on them.

"Cars aren't silly," she'd sniffled.

"Edsels are," he'd assured her.

She hadn't been convinced, but she'd worn the socks—for a while. He'd gotten a call from the school sometime later—Jill's socks were uncomfortable because they were too big. Could he possibly bring her a pair of her own to wear? He'd had to shut up the garage, run home and grab socks to take to school.

In the process, he'd discovered that Lexie was digging holes all over the backyard, including several suspiciously near the fence. He'd have reinforce that boundary soon, maybe install one of those invisible fences with the training collars that administered a shock.

Or maybe not. Josh would never stand for that, Patrick was fairly certain.

"You comin' in?" Ruby was standing on the front porch of the center, her hands on her bony hips.

"Yes, ma'am." He got out of the truck and headed up the path.

"You're late," she informed him.

"Sorry. It's been a...challenging day."

The older woman's face remained solemn but understanding twinkled in her eyes. "Parenting's full of days like that. Don't I remember! While I got you to myself, I want to talk about that little arrangement you and me had. Don't seem to me like you're holding up your end of the bargain."

He felt a twinge of irritation. "I'm doing what I can, Ruby."

"Are you? Near as I can tell, you two have been joined at the hip just lately. Going up Big Pig, adopting dogs, getting lost in corn mazes together."

"We didn't get lost. And Torey's a grown woman

with a mind of her own. I can't very well tell her where she can and can't go. With all due respect, you're the one who wanted us to run this center together, so—"

"What are you two talking about?" Torey opened the front door and looked them over suspiciously. "The kids are going to be here before long, so if Ruby's going to pick the float design secretly, she'd better do it."

"True enough," Ruby agreed without a blink. "Let's go see what these children have come up with."

The art teacher had dedicated an entire wall to the float design suggestions. Pictures were tacked up on a yellow background, depicting various types of floats. At least Patrick assumed they were floats—some of the smaller kids' artwork required a lot of imagination.

That didn't deter Ruby. The elderly woman made her way down the hallway, giving each picture its due attention. Torey and Patrick had decided to allow Ruby to choose, knowing that the children were less likely to dispute her decision—and that she'd choose wisely.

So they stood awkwardly together at the end of the hallway waiting. Patrick stole little glances in Torey's direction. She stood with her arms crossed, carefully not looking at him. She was more dressed up today than usual, wearing a slim dark pantsuit with a creamy blouse. Her hair was pulled into a sleek coil, and even her earrings were formal, silver disks without much dangle to them.

It was a contrast to the Torey he'd seen yesterday at Jorgeson's. She'd been wearing a sunshine-yellow blouse and a long denim skirt with brown, buttery-looking boots, and earrings of twisted silver and turquoise.

She'd looked…pretty. And warm and friendly and fun. He remembered the little jolt he'd felt when she'd walked in his direction. He sneaked another look at her. She was aware of him watching. He read that in the stiff way she was standing, and the way her fingers drummed on her biceps. But she wouldn't look at him.

He'd hurt her feelings yesterday, snapping at her about his dad. He shouldn't have. He'd been thrown for a loop when his father had shown up—and a little irritated with Torey for telling Ron where to find him. He'd wanted to make it crystal clear that she wasn't going to soften him up where his dad was concerned. There was too much at stake.

But he could have been a little nicer about it.

"This one." Ruby pointed to a picture in the middle of the display.

"Are you sure?" Torey asked. They walked over to inspect her choice.

"Positive. I've looked 'em all over, and this is the one. A Hopeful Harvest—that's a real nice name for a float. And see, you've got yourself a little garden, with all these vegetables coming up. Only they ain't only vegetables, they're the things we're trying to teach the young'uns here. See? Honesty, Kindness, and Self-Control. Yes, this is the one all right."

"All right." Torey unpinned the drawing. "Well, that's decided." She lifted an eyebrow at Patrick. "It's got a tractor on it and a barn with lights. Think your engine class can pull that off?"

"I'm sure we can."

Ruby chuckled. "I like a man with confidence. 'Course, building a float ain't nothing compared to taking two children on to raise, all by your lonesome."

"I'll scan this into my computer and email it to you so we'll each have a copy to work with." Torey disappeared into the director's office. He watched her go, thinking that her dark suit might be stylish, but it wasn't particularly cheerful.

"All right," Ruby said. "What's going on, Patrick? You look like you got something on your mind."

*I'm wishing Torey had worn that pretty yellow shirt—and maybe the jeans she wore when we went up to Big Pig. And that she'd smile at me again like she did at Jorgeson's before my dad showed up.*

He couldn't say that. So instead, he said, "It's been a tough day. I've been dropping some balls—

like I forgot it was a special sock day at Jill's school, and she got upset."

Ruby made a sympathetic noise. "Them schools are always coming up with something like that. Sock day, hat day, backwards day. Seems like it's always something. It's a lot to keep up with," she said. "'Specially for a fellow like you."

Patrick remembered what the woman had said back in the corn maze, about how Josh might relate better to his mom right now. If only he *had* a mom. "So, you think a woman could do a better job?" he asked.

Ruby sputtered. "I didn't say any such thing. I meant because you got a business to run, too. It's a lot on your plate." She tilted her head, looking at him like a curious, gray bird. "Having second thoughts about being a single parent?"

"No. I don't know. Maybe." Patrick ran a hand through his hair. "I'm doing my best, but I'm not sure it's good enough. I'm not sure I'm what the kids need."

"What those kids need is somebody who won't give up on them when things get hard." Torey spoke from the office, her voice sharp. "Somebody who's there no matter what, no matter how hard it gets, no matter what mistakes they make. If you can't be that person, then maybe you do need to reconsider fostering. And certainly adoption."

She turned and disappeared into the office, banging the door shut behind herself.

"Adoption?" Ruby asked. Without waiting for an answer, she shook her head. "My, my, my. Well, that's a big step. I can see why you're second-guessing yourself."

"That makes one of you," Patrick muttered, sending another glance toward the closed door.

"Torey could've been more polite. But you know how important loyalty is to her, particularly when it comes to family. She didn't get any of that from her mama growing up, so it means that much more to her."

"My dad showed up at the farm yesterday," Patrick heard himself saying. The rest of the story slipped out as Ruby listened attentively. When he'd finished, she sighed.

"Ron Callahan's sweet as sugar and slippery as butter. I've always said so. He has some really bad timing, too."

"Could have been worse. At least the social worker wasn't there."

"That's not what I meant," Ruby muttered. "Sounds like you and Torey been tromping on each other's sore spots. I'll let you in on a little secret. We've got three interviews lined up for the center director job. If you want to make up and end this on a good note, you'd better do it while you can. She'll be heading back down to Atlanta anytime now. Why don't you go talk to her? Smooth things over, so to speak?" She gave him a nudge with her elbow.

Patrick sent another look at the door. As he considered, Ruby gave him another little poke. "Kids going to be getting off the bus pretty soon," she pointed out. "Won't be no privacy to be had then."

He gave in. "All right." He walked to the door and knocked.

"Come in," Torey's voice was muffled through the heavy wood.

He cracked the door open. She was seated at her desk, working on her laptop. When she saw him looking in, she sighed.

"Can we talk?" he asked.

"Sure." She closed the laptop, sitting up straighter in the chair he'd fixed for her.

"It wasn't your fault my dad followed us out to the farm yesterday. I'm sorry I was short with you."

"Well, while we're apologizing, I'm sorry, too, Patrick. I shouldn't have snapped at you back there."

"That's okay," he started, but she shook her head.

"No, it isn't. My family knows better than most how hard fostering can be. And I'm not the one doing it, so I have no right to criticize."

He sank down into the metal chair across from the desk. "Maybe you have more right than most to criticize because you understand the situation from the inside out. And believe me, I already know I'm not perfect."

"You don't have to be perfect to love people. You just have to do one thing."

He waited, but she didn't say anything else. "And what's that?" he prompted finally.

"I told you already." She leaned forward over her closed computer, her eyes intense. "Never. Give. Up."

"Hello?" A woman's voice called from outside.

"That's Charlotte." Torey stood up. "She and Ruby are going to help get the kids started on making their costumes for the parade float. We're thinking some flowers and vegetables, maybe some seed packets, and of course a farmer and a scarecrow. You said you were handling all the moving parts and getting a trailer and a truck to pull it, right?"

"What?" Patrick blinked. "Right. Yeah. I have all that covered."

"Great. We'll talk later, then." She edged her way around him and went out to greet her sister-in-law.

He stayed where he was, thinking hard. After a second or two, he took out his phone and punched in Mitzi's office number.

"Put me on your schedule," he told her when she picked up. "As soon as you can. And ask Mrs. Darnell to sit in. We need to talk."

# Chapter Nine

A few days later, Patrick locked his garage an hour earlier than usual and drove to the Department of Family and Children's Services.

"So?" Mitzi asked after they were seated in a small conference room. "What's the problem?" She tapped on her laptop, angling it so that her supervisor could also see the screen. "Joshua and Jill Pruitt," she murmured. "Has Josh been involved in another incident at school?"

"No," Patrick said. "Josh has been doing fine. We got a dog, and that's been a real help. The school hasn't reported any problems since he went back, and I'm keeping in touch with his teachers. Jill's doing great, too. I'm volunteering over at the Hope Center—"

"Oh, good!" Mrs. Darnell interjected.

"I'm teaching a couple of classes on engines there, and we've got art classes and sewing classes and—" He hesitated, but he'd decided to be completely honest in this meeting. "A computer lab up and running." He swallowed, realizing complete honesty demanded that he say something else. "Josh had a little blip with that, and he was put on computer restriction for a while."

"A little blip," Mitzi repeated ominously.

"He accessed a computer game he wasn't supposed to. But he apologized, and it was handled. Torey Bryant—she's the codirector I'm working with—knows all about computers, so she nipped that in the bud and made sure it wouldn't happen again. Also, we've recruited some local pastors and a counselor from the school, and they're doing mini workshops with the kids on topics like internet safety, anger management, bullying, study habits, and stuff like that."

Mrs. Darnell was beaming. "That sounds wonderful! I can't tell you how happy I am to hear that the Hope Center is thriving again. It's a muchneeded resource in this community, especially for the families we serve. Don't you agree, Mitzi?"

"I do." Mitzi sounded reserved and slightly suspicious. "But if everything's going well with the children and the Hope Center, why are we here?"

He swallowed. Time to turn over this engine and see what happened. "I want to talk to you about adopting Josh and Jill myself."

"Oh." The two women exchanged a glance.

Mrs. Darnell murmured something to Mitzi, who quickly clicked a few keys on the laptop and pushed it closer to her boss. The supervisor frowned as she read something on the screen.

"You're listed as strictly foster, not foster-to-adopt, Patrick."

"It's my understanding that can be changed fairly easily."

"It can." She leaned back in her chair and studied him. "But a change like that is something I need to understand very thoroughly. Why do you want to adopt these children?"

Mitzi cleared her throat. "This is his first placement, and you know how first-time foster parents get. They become attached, and—"

"Thank you, Mitzi. And yes, I'm aware of all that. But I'd like to hear what Patrick has to say. You're a single parent."

"Yes, I am."

"That's a demanding job. Especially with children who have traumas and challenges."

"Yes, it is."

"Do you have a…" the older woman hesitated, "a significant other in your life? A girlfriend? Someone you could see yourself in a long-term relationship with?"

"Um." He wasn't sure why Torey's face popped into his mind, or why he stuttered answering such a simple, straightforward question. "I'm not dating anybody right now." That was truthful, he reminded himself. "But I was told single people could adopt."

"They can. But as you just admitted, being a single parent is a difficult job. Granted, it's a job many men and women do every day. Some by necessity, some by choice, and with varying degrees of success. Many of the children we serve come from overwhelmed single parent families, so I'm all too familiar with the challenges."

"I was raised by a single dad. So I am, too."

"I see. Well, that certainly gives you a model to follow, assuming it was a positive experience. Do you have a good relationship with your father?"

Before he could answer, Mitzi cleared her throat. "His father was incarcerated for a number of years. Remember? The chop shop thing?"

"Oh!" Mrs. Darnell nodded slowly. "You're Ron Callahan's son."

"That's right. And no, my father and I haven't been...close...for quite some time because I didn't agree with his choices." He sat up straighter in his chair. "Look, Mrs. Darnell, I'm not a perfect man, and I certainly don't come from a perfect background. Far from it. My father's not the only relative who's seen the inside of a prison. Some people—" he had to work to keep his gaze from slipping to Mitzi "—some people think that's a big negative. Maybe it is, in a way. But I'll tell you this. My family history helps me understand where these kids come from. I'm familiar with the challenges that come from having parents and cousins and aunts and uncles who make bad choices. And I know the kind of grit you need to pull yourself out of that lifestyle when it's all you've ever known. I may not be able to help Josh too much with computers or Jill with her hair, although I'll try. But I can help them learn how to do that. And I want to."

"I admire that," Mrs. Darnell said. "But—"

He couldn't allow any *but*s. "Mitzi here wants to split these kids up. She thinks she should send Josh to a group home and find a family to adopt Jill."

"It's not ideal," Mitzi said hurriedly. "But considering the available resources, it's our best option. I'm trying to find a family who will take both children, but—"

"I understand," her supervisor interrupted wearily. She turned her attention back to Patrick. "I've been in this business quite a while, and I can tell you, it's very difficult to find an adoptive family for sibling groups. Boys are harder to place than girls. The older the child is, the more difficult it is to find a placement. When you factor in a child with documented behavioral problems—"

"Lots of them," Mitzi interjected.

"Then," Mrs. Darnell continued as if her coworker hadn't spoken, "finding a family changes from difficult to nearly impossible."

"Not for Josh and Jill, it's not. I'll take them both."

A silence fell over the table, and Patrick held his breath.

"All right," Mrs. Darnell said.

Patrick's breath rushed out in a whoosh. "Thank you! I promise—"

She held up a hand. "Wait. I'm only agreeing that you can do the paperwork to change your status and that we'll look into the possibility of you adopting the children. It's on the table, but at the moment, that's all. Understood?"

"Understood. And if there's anything I can do to tip the scales in my favor, I'm more than willing to do it."

"Well, a minute ago you mentioned that there were some aspects of parenting Josh and Jill that you were struggling with. Josh's computer misbehavior and Jill's hair. Not uncommon, of course. All single parents have areas that they're just not that skilled in. What's important is that you seek out help in those areas. To be a strong single parent, you're going to need a strong support system. When you're fostering, of course, we provide some of that support. But once these children are legally yours, that support diminishes. And you'll still need help—more than ever. So," she said, rising to her feet. "That would be my recommendation. Keep doing what you're doing, but seek out help in the areas that you're lacking in. In the meantime, Mitzi will get you started on the necessary paperwork."

"Thanks. I'll do that. And I promise, I'll try my very best for these kids."

Mrs. Darnell smiled. "I think you will. You're right, Patrick. You're not perfect. Nobody is. But that grit you mentioned, and the determination that brought you into this office today, along with your willingness to make a permanent commitment to these children...those things may very well swing the balance in your favor." She held out her hand for him to shake. "With fostering, we're looking for parents who can love children for a time and then gracefully let them go when their circumstances change. With adoption, we're looking for parents who will stick with a kid through thick and thin, no matter what. You seem to fit the bill, so we'll see what we can do."

On the drive home, Patrick mulled over the meeting, trying to keep his growing excitement in check. Adopting Josh and Jill was a real possibility.

Of course, he couldn't say anything to the kids. Not yet. There'd been enough broken promises in their lives already, and a lot of this was out of his control.

On the other hand, some of it he could control—and he'd meant what he'd said back in the DFCS office. He'd make a list of the things he was struggling with, and he'd start building that support system Mrs. Darnell had mentioned.

Funny that she'd talked about sticking with

kids through thick and thin. Torey had made a point of that as well. Over the years, Patrick had learned to pay attention when something like that kept coming up. Sometimes God was trying to get a point across.

*I won't give up on Josh and Jill, Lord,* he prayed as he drove. "*No matter what. And if there are... other relationships you want me to stick with, just let me know. My dad or...someone else. Just...be clear enough, please, so that I can't misunderstand. Okay? Because I don't trust my judgment, and I really can't afford to make any mistakes right now.*

He left the prayer there, delicately balanced between hope and uncertainty. Another thing he'd learned over the years was to leave this kind of request with God. It was like soaking engine parts to make them easier to clean. You couldn't rush that. You had to give it time.

Of course, every now and then, God surprised you with a speedy answer. So, maybe he shouldn't have been so startled when he pulled up at the Hope Center and saw Torey on the front porch.

Talking with his father.

When Torey saw Patrick's truck, her heart dipped. She'd been doing her best to shoo Ron Callahan away before Patrick arrived, but the older man had proved immune to her hints.

Clearly he planned to stay right where he was until he had a conversation with his son.

As Patrick mounted the steps, Torey sent him a look. "Your dad stopped by," she said, doing her best to convey *and I had nothing to do with it.*

"Hi there, son." Ron spoke with a cheerfulness that didn't reach his eyes. "I stopped by the garage, but when I saw it was closed again, I figured you'd be here. Thought maybe you and I could have that talk."

"Excuse me," an irritated voice called from the sidewalk. Barton Myers was striding in their direction. "It was the neighborhood's understanding that there wouldn't be a great deal of vehicle traffic at this center. Now there's an immense trailer parked in your backyard—"

"That's for the Harvest Parade. It won't be there long." And it wasn't visible from the street, so Torey didn't see why it was a problem. It likely wouldn't be for anyone but Barton.

"Not only that," the man went on, "but three vehicles are parked in front of this house, Miss Bryant. Three. And one of them is a derelict." He pointed at Ron's truck.

Ron studied the other man with a furrowed brow. "A say-what?"

"A derelict," he repeated.

Ron snorted. "That ain't no derelict, mister. That's a '56 Chevy. And it belongs to me."

"It's an eyesore, and it shouldn't be parked on this street."

Ron crossed his arms and leaned against the porch banister. "Don't see why not. It's got a legal tag. It needs a paint job, but if that bothers you, you ain't got to look at it."

Barton rummaged in his pocket for a notepad. "What is your name, sir?"

"Ron Callahan. That's C-A-L-L-A—

"The truck'll be gone in a minute, Mr. Myers," Torey cut in quickly.

"It better be." He swept all three of them with a glare and stalked down the sidewalk, cramming the notebook back into his pocket.

"Who's that fussbudget?" Ron asked.

"Never mind him. What do you want, Dad?"

"I told you already. To talk to you. For just a minute," he added. "Then I'll leave."

Torey watched Patrick think it over. He glanced at her, and their eyes met. To her surprise, the firm line of his jaw softened.

"Okay, but we don't have long. We're working on a parade float, and we're going to have a bus-load of overexcited kids here in about…" Patrick checked his watch, "ten minutes."

"If ten minutes is all you got, I'll take it." Ron took a deep breath. "Listen, son—"

She had no business listening to this conversation. "Excuse me. I'll go inside."

"No. Stay. Please," Patrick added. "I'd like you

to hear this. I think it's important that we all be on the same page."

That sounded ominous. Torey threw a sympathetic look in Ron's direction. "All right."

"Say whatever it is you want to say, Dad. Just try to keep it short.

"I can say what I need to say in two words. I've changed. I don't expect you to believe me. You got your reasons not to, and I respect that. But I'd like to ask you for just one more opportunity to prove it to you. Just one."

Ron's voice was steady, but his hands trembled, and Torey found herself praying that Patrick's heart would soften.

His eyes sought hers again, and he ran a hand through his hair, standing it on end. "I don't know, Dad. What are you thinking that would look like?"

Ron's eyes lit up. "Whatever you're willing to allow. I could… I could help you, some, maybe. Now you got the kids, I've noticed you closing the garage more. I could lend a hand there, help you keep your business going."

Patrick's expression chilled. "I don't think so."

Ron swallowed. "I deserve that. Well, it don't have to be there. Anything you need a hand with, I'll pitch in. I'd just like to…spend some time with you. Show you I can be trusted. Because I can, now."

Torey held her breath, watching Patrick think it over.

"Just one shot, son. That's all I'm asking. If I blow this, I won't be back asking for another one."

Patrick ruffled his hair again, a sure sign he was agitated. Finally, he seemed to come to a decision. "Dad, I'm going to lay this out for you. I've got a lot on the line now. I have two kids I'm looking after and a business to run, and I'm helping out at this center."

"I'm proud of you. You've really made something of yourself."

"My point is, I have a lot to lose. So if I let you back into my life, it's going to be little by little, and it's going to be on my terms. Is that understood?

Ron was already nodding. "You just tell me when to show up and I'll be there." He rummaged in a pocket and came out with a slip of paper. "This here's got my number on it. You can call me anytime, day or night."

Patrick accepted the paper. "All right. Thanks. The kids are going to be here any minute, so you'd better get going."

Ron's happy expression dimmed, but he nodded. "Okay. Don't lose that piece of paper, now. Torey-My-Glory, it was good to see you, like always."

Torey swallowed the lump that was forming in her throat. "Good to see you, too, Ron."

She and Patrick stood together on the porch, watching until Ron backed his old pickup out of the driveway and rumbled down the street.

When he was finally out of sight, Patrick blew out a tired sigh. "How long had he been here before I drove up?"

"Not long. Fifteen minutes, maybe."

"You didn't leave him alone in the house, did you? If you did, you'd better count the spoons."

"We use plastic spoons, so I think we're good." When Patrick didn't smile, she added, "He wasn't alone in the house. I met him on the porch, and we stayed out here."

"Good. Make sure he never is alone in the house. Not even for five minutes. And please don't tell him my schedule or any details about the kids, either."

"I won't." Torey watched as Patrick crumpled up the slip of paper. He tossed it into the trash can they'd set on the porch for the kids to throw away the food and drinks they weren't supposed to bring into the center.

He caught her eye. "Relax. I already have his number on my phone from when he called me before. I made sure I added him to my contacts. I didn't want to be caught by surprise again."

"Are you going to call him?"

"I'm going to think about it."

Torey wanted to say more, but she clamped her lips shut and remained silent. This was dangerous ground, and she'd dodged enough bullets where Ron Callahan was concerned already.

"You're about to chew your tongue in two, aren't you?" Patrick chuckled wearily. "Well, you don't have to say it. I already know what you think."

"Well," Torey said, unable to resist, "if you don't want him around the garage—"

"I don't."

"Maybe he could help you here with the float. He's a good mechanic. You were saying that getting the tractor and the lights and everything to move like the kids want would be a challenge."

"I don't think that's a good idea, Torey."

"It would make him feel included, and it would be a short-term thing. Plus, this is neutral territory."

"Nothing's neutral with my family." He sighed again. "Back when we were dating, I sheltered you from the worst of it, but trust me, the Callahans are nothing but trouble. They'll charm your socks off and then steal everything that's not nailed down the minute your back's turned. I thought my father was different, but it turned out he wasn't."

"Maybe he is now."

"Maybe." Patrick looked doubtful. "But I can't be sure, and the stakes are a lot higher now. I just came from a meeting over at the social services office. I talked to Mitzi and Mrs. Darnell about adopting Josh and Jill. They agreed to start the paperwork."

"*Seriously?*" Before she thought better of it, she threw her arms around him and gave him a fierce, hard hug. "Oh, Patrick, that's wonderful!"

For a second he stood stock-still. Then his arms went around her, pressing her close. Memories washed over her in a warm shower. She closed her eyes and breathed in the scent of him—the faint scent of metal and leather combined with that ever-present whiff of oranges. Then he released her and took a step back.

"The bus." His voice sounded strangely gruff. "It just turned onto the street."

"Oh!" This was embarrassing. "Sorry. I didn't mean anything by that. I was just—so happy for you."

"Well, thanks, but there's still a long way to go. They're starting the paperwork to move me into the foster-to-adopt category, but they were clear that nothing's for certain." He cleared his throat. "There…uh…was one thing I wanted to ask you about."

"What's that?"

"They suggested that I'd need to line up some resources. As a single parent, it's pretty hard to cover all the bases. I was thinking about Josh's fascination with computers and what you said about him being a prodigy and all that. I wanted to ask for a favor."

Her heart beat faster. "Sure. Anything."

"I need somebody who knows computers to help with what you were talking about. Guiding him, helping him use his skills in the right way."

"I think that's a great idea."

"I wondered if you'd connect me with one of your friends who knows about that kind of stuff. Somebody local or at least not too far away."

"Oh." It was ridiculous how deflated she felt. "Well, sure, I can try to think of somebody. Or," she offered hesitantly, "I could do it myself. If you'd be comfortable with that."

He looked at her for a second, then away, toward the yellow bus easing up the street.

"It's nice of you to offer, and if you want to do some mentoring while you're here, that'd be great. But you'll be moving back to Atlanta soon, so I'll need somebody else for the long term."

"Oh. Right." She'd be moving back to Atlanta. Weird how she kept forgetting that. And, she realized suddenly, she'd never answered her boss's last email.

Or the previous one. She'd better do that. Immediately.

"Okay. I'll help for the time being, and I'm sure I can come up with somebody else for…later."

"Thanks."

"You're welcome."

"No, seriously, Torey." He looked down at her,

his blue-green eyes filled with a gentleness that felt heartbreakingly familiar. "Thank you."

Before she could answer, the kids poured off the bus and swarmed up the porch, surrounding them with demands to get started on the float. Torey laughed as they crowded close, tugging at her, all of them talking at once.

"All right, all right," she heard Patrick saying. "Everybody to the backyard!"

The sea of children squealed and thundered off the porch, dragging Patrick with them. He glanced over his shoulder. "You coming? Or do you have something else to do?"

Torey thought of the unanswered emails then pushed them recklessly out of her mind.

"Not a thing," she said. "Let's go make a float."

# Chapter Ten

On Saturday evening Patrick finished double-checking the wiring on the float that was supposed to make the barn lights twinkle and the tractor wheels turn. He didn't see any problems.

Of course, they'd been working on this thing all week, and so far he'd learned two things. One, floats were a lot harder to pull together than you'd think, and two, just because you didn't see any problems didn't mean there weren't any.

"Okay." He raised his voice to be heard over the chatter of a dozen elementary school students who were helping the art teacher arrange papier-mâché' vegetables on the bed of the trailer. "Flip the switch!"

One of the boys must have complied. There was a buzzing noise, and the lights sparkled to life. The tractor wheels began whirling, and the crew of tired children and teachers broke into relieved applause.

There was an ominous rattle. The lights blinked, then dimmed back into darkness. A disappointed groan came from the group.

"Mr. Patrick, if the lights aren't on, people won't be able to see the float too good," a little girl reminded him. "We got to have lights."

"Don't worry. We'll have plenty of lights," he assured her. "I hope," he added under his breath.

He sat back on his heels and surveyed the float. Hours of effort had transformed his flatbed trailer into a vegetable garden. It was pretty cute. It was also amazing how hard these kids had worked, and they'd even turned up for an extra session today.

He'd worked hard, too, but everything that could go wrong on his end, had. He was starting to have nightmares about this thing.

In none of those dreams did the lights work.

"Time for a coffee break." Torey paused beside him, holding out a mug.

"Thanks."

"How's it going?"

"Not great, and this thing's got to be ready to go tomorrow afternoon," he said. "We've got more problems than I can shake a stick at. I'm worried the kids are going to be disappointed."

"I'm not worried. You'll figure it out," Torey said. "You always do. You'll think better after you've had your coffee." She smiled at him, then jumped off the float and walked back to

he house, her dark ponytail bouncing underneath
ier ball cap.

He watched her go, realizing belatedly that he
vas smiling. He blinked and took a sip of his cof-
'ee. No sugar, one dollop of cream, and piping
1ot, just the way he liked it.

But when he caught sight of Josh, sitting alone
)n the porch steps, his smile faded. He climbed
)ff the float, careful not to spill his coffee. He
1eeded all the caffeine he could get.

"Hi," he said, dropping down on the cold brick
;tep.

"How much longer are we going to be stuck
1ere?" Josh demanded.

"A while," Patrick said. "I'm having trouble
3etting the moving parts on the float to work. I
:ould use some help once I finish this coffee, if
/ou're game."

"I don't know anything about all that stuff."

"You don't have to. I can tell you what to do."
At least he hoped he could. Once he figured out
vhat that was.

Josh's only response was a sigh.

"If you'd rather help somebody else, that's fine.
There's plenty left to do."

"Whatever."

It had been a long day, and Patrick felt his frus-
ration gaining ground. He tried his best to tamp
t back down.

"Look," he said, keeping his voice level. "We

had a deal, right? You'd participate in this with a good attitude, and we'd cut your computer suspension to two weeks. I'm assuming you still want that deal, but I'm not seeing a great attitude here. Or much participation."

"I'm participating." Josh reached down on the step beside him and held up a tin bucket with a spatter of autumn leaves painted on the side. "I got to walk in the parade tomorrow and carry this thing and hand out candy. Ain't that enough?"

He sounded disgusted.

"It sounds like fun."

"It's dumb."

"Handing out candy to kids is dumb? It's really not, Josh. We used to throw it from the floats, but this way there's less risk of a little kid running out into the road after a piece of candy and getting hurt."

Josh shot him a sideways look. "Well, maybe it's not as dumb as I thought, then. But there's lots of other kids handing out the candy. They barely had enough buckets to go around. I don't see why I have to do it, too."

"You don't." Torey spoke from above them. She had a couple of empty coffee cups dangling from her fingers. "Not if there's something else you'd rather do. Is there?"

"Stay home and play with Lexie."

Torey smiled. "How's the little escape artist doing?"

Josh's face lit up. "A lot better. We got her a harness thing to wear so she can't slip her collar no more. She walks real good on her leash now."

"That's great!" Torey looked at Patrick. She lifted her eyebrows and nodded toward Josh.

Patrick frowned. She obviously wanted him to say something, but he had no idea what. "Yeah," he said slowly. "Lexie's doing really well, and Josh has been working hard with her."

"Do you think she could handle walking in the parade?" Torey asked.

Josh jumped to his feet. "I know she could! Seriously, Miss Torey, could she?"

"That's up to your dad."

"Paddy, could she? She never slips loose no more! And if she got tired, she could ride on the float, or I could pull that wagon you got for Jill. Lexie loves riding in that."

"I don't see why not." Patrick marveled at the change in Josh's expression. Smart move on Torey's part, bringing the dog into this. He should have thought of that. He was planning to walk alongside the float himself, so if there was a problem with the dog, he could easily step in.

And he hadn't missed the fact that Josh had called him *Paddy*.

"People love dogs," Torey said. "And Lexie's such a beauty. She'll be a great attention getter." She cocked her head at the boy. "You'll probably have to talk to a lot of folks. Be friendly, and all that."

"I won't mind. I could tell them about how we adopted her. And maybe they'd go and adopt another dog and give her a better life like we did Lexie. Do you think they might?"

"They might, Josh." Patrick agreed, his heart swelling. "They just might."

"I could give them a card, maybe. With a phone number to the dog rescue place. I could print those out tonight. Please, could I? That way I could give them out with the candy. I know I'm not supposed to use the computer, but couldn't I just use it long enough to make the cards?"

"I can make them for you," Torey offered. "You write down everything you want it to say, and I'll mock it up real quick. You can have final approval, and we'll make any changes you want. Then we'll print them off."

"Here." Patrick pulled out his wallet. He rummaged until he found the scrap of paper where he'd scribbled the name of the animal rescue foundation Ed volunteered for, along with its phone number and website. "I think that's all the information you'll need."

"Thanks!" Josh said. "I'll get some paper and pencil and write everything just like it needs to be on the card. We should put a picture of a dog on it, too." He climbed the steps and started in the back door.

"Paper's in the art room," Torey called. She dropped down on the step beside Patrick and set the empty mugs between them. "I hope that was all right," she said. "The dog thing."

"Are you kidding? It was brilliant. I couldn't get him interested in anything to do with this parade, but his attitude did a one-eighty the minute you mentioned including Lexie. He's nuts about that dog."

"He is." She gave him a sidelong look that did funny things to his heartbeat. "He's a lot like you that way."

"I like dogs. But I don't think I've ever liked one as much as Josh loves Lexie."

"Not what I meant. It's not really the dog, is it? It's taking care of the dog that makes her special to him. He likes to look after things. Dogs. People. You two have more in common than you think."

Patrick thought it over. "You might be right. Josh has looked after Jill for years. I had a hard time getting him to let me do anything for her at first. And he's sure devoted to Lexie."

Torey smiled. "I'm right about you, too. You've been taking care of people as long as I've known you. It's your specialty, trying to fix them, like you fix those old cars you like so much."

"That doesn't always work out so well. Fixing the people," he added. "I've got a better track record with the cars."

"Fixing people's not really our job, anyway," Torey pointed out. "Ruby says we're just supposed to love them and leave the fixing up to God."

He leaned back against the steps. "Why do I get the feeling we're talking about my dad?"

Torey grinned. "Because we are."

"I gave up trying to fix my father—or anybody else in my family—a long time ago."

"Probably a smart move." She leaned back too, stretching her legs over the short grass. "I like Ron, but I have to admit, I'm not fond of some of your cousins."

He stiffened and looked at her. "You've met my cousins?"

"Only two of them, and only once. Thankfully."

"Which two? And when?" He was sitting upright on the steps now. He'd taken care—a lot of care—that Torey never had any contact with his family, aside from his dad, whom he considered harmless. He didn't know what she was talking about, but he already knew he didn't like it.

"They said their names were Joe and Dwayne." She looked at him, her brow furrowed. "Relax. I'm talking about something that happened a long time ago, Patrick. Back when we were dating."

*Something that happened.* He knew Joe and Dwayne. Nothing involving them was ever good news. He felt his blood go cold.

"What happened, Torey?"

"Nothing important."

"Torey."

She made a frustrated noise. "It was silly, really. Scary but silly. They cornered me one day when I was coming out of school."

He was on his feet so fast that he startled her, making her bump herself on the metal stair railing. "They did *what?*"

"Patrick, calm down! It was ten years ago."

"Did they put their hands on you? Did they hurt you?"

"No. Now, sit back down. Seriously, before you have an audience of kids over here wanting to know what's going on."

She was right. Already a few heads were swiveling in his direction. He dropped back down on the steps. "Tell me what they did."

"Why? What are you going to do? Go hunt them down after all these years?"

Well, yeah. Maybe. "I want to know, Torey."

She blew out a sigh. "They got out of an El Camino on my way to the parking lot and crowded me up against a van. Said some ugly things, threatened me, told me to tell you to back off with the court case or else."

He felt like he was going to throw up. "That's it?" Not that it wasn't enough, but with Joe and Dwayne, it could have been a lot worse. "Then they just let you go?"

She smirked. "They didn't have much choice. I'd spent years in foster care, and I had three brand-new brothers who'd made sure I knew how to defend myself. I also had a backpack full of honors textbooks. I left them some bruises to remember me by."

"You should have told me."

"Going by your reaction now, I'm glad I didn't. You might have ended up in jail right alongside your dad. That could've been what they were hoping for. The fact that they wanted me to tell you sent up some flares. I was stubborn enough not to do what they told me. But I'd have let you know if they'd tried anything else. I figured they might, but they didn't. Of course, not long after that we broke up, so—"

"I'm sorry." He wasn't really paying attention to what she was saying. He was thinking and fuming. "I'm so sorry that happened to you, Torey. It was my fault. I should have broken up with you sooner. I knew it, but I kept putting it off, and—"

"What do you mean?"

The sharpness of her voice cut into his thoughts, and he blinked.

"Nothing," he said quickly.

"Patrick Callahan, did you break up with me because you were afraid your family was going to hurt me?"

"Sounds like they nearly did, Torey. Joe and

Dwayne are both in prison now, and they have a string of convictions as long as your arm. Things could have gone a lot worse that day."

"It had nothing to do with what I did," Torey murmured. Her face had gone pale. "But you let me think that because you—"

"Torey," he started, but she shook her head.

"No. Now's not the time. We'd better not open that can of worms right now."

"Agreed," he said with a sense of relief.

"For now," she went on, giving him a sharp look. "We're definitely talking about it later. But tonight, we have other stuff to deal with."

An uneasy silence fell as they studied the hive of activity in front of them. They'd positioned the float just under the backyard security light, helpful now that dusk was falling. The air was full of the chatter of excited kids, and the smell of construction paper and glue, mingled with coffee and the pizza they'd treated the kids to an hour ago.

"You know, when I came here a few weeks ago, this place was dead as a doornail, and now look at it. I think this is working," Torey said quietly. "It's really working."

She seemed calm enough now. Patrick relaxed a little. "Thanks to you."

"Thanks to both of us." She drew in a breath. "And no thanks to Barton Myers. He called a while ago, threatening to phone in a noise complaint if we're out here working past ten."

Patrick groaned. "I'd better get back to that float, then. No telling how long it's going to take to get everything working. If I even can."

But he didn't budge. He felt reluctant to leave her side. Hearing about her near miss all those years ago had revved up all kinds of protective instincts and…other feelings…that he'd put on ice. Surprisingly, they felt just as fresh and strong as they always had. The problem was, he had no idea what to do with them.

"You know, the work would probably move faster if you had some quality help," Torey said.

"You offering?"

She grinned. "We both know about how much help I'd be." She paused. "I do know somebody who might be able to help, though. And he did offer." She raised her eyebrows.

"I see we're back to talking about my dad."

"Can't get anything by you." Torey gave his forearm a squeeze. "Give him a chance, Patrick. That's all he's asked for." She smiled. "See for yourself if God's been doing some fixing over the past few years."

He started to say no. Not now. Maybe not ever, but definitely not now. He'd thought it through, sitting at home with Lexie snoring at his feet and the kids safely asleep in their clean, warm beds.

He was close to having everything he'd ever wanted. He felt suddenly conscious of Torey sitting beside him, of how she'd left a careful distance between them.

Well. Almost everything. Now was not the time to take risks. He started to tell her that.

But then he glanced over and caught Torey's eye, felt the warmth of her fingers on his arm.

And against his better judgment, he reached for his phone.


On the day of the parade, Torey scanned the clear sky and breathed a prayer of gratitude. The Sunday afternoon was crisp and clear, which meant that there would be no soggy crepe paper disasters on the float.

Which was good, because there were plenty of other disasters. She and Patrick had been putting out fires ever since they'd arrived at the high school football field parking lot where the parade was being staged. Right now, he and his father had their heads buried in a large diesel truck's engine, trying to get the thing to start.

Because if it didn't, they weren't going to have a way to pull the float.

"Turn 'er over," Ron barked. Josh, sitting alongside Lexie in the cab of the truck, twisted the key, producing a painful grinding sound. "Okay, stop! See right there?" Ron pointed out something in the depths of the engine to Patrick. "That's the problem."

"Yeah." Patrick leaned farther into the engine,

until only the toes of his boots were touching the pavement. Since he planned to drive the truck pulling the float, he was wearing denim overalls, so at least it wouldn't matter much if he got dirty.

"Careful," Ron warned.

"I know what I'm doing, Dad." Patrick sounded half irritated, half amused.

She liked seeing the two of them working together again, just like the old days. On countless afternoons she'd watched them disemboweling some engine, bickering good-naturedly.

She'd argued with Patrick over his decision to cut Ron out of his life. She didn't open her heart to people easily back then. Patrick had been an exception. But pretty soon she'd fallen for Ron, too. She'd never had a dad, and he'd filled that spot—not perfectly, but kindly. She knew he'd done wrong, but she'd never even met her own dad—and her bio mom couldn't have cared less about her. She didn't understand how Patrick could turn his back on a father who actually cared about him. About both of them.

But he had. So, it had seemed believable later when Patrick had cut her out of his life, too. She was still trying to wrap her head around the fact that he'd done that—at least partly—because he was worried about her, not just because she'd changed his test score.

Maybe that should have made her feel better. It didn't. It irritated her because it meant all that heartbreak had been pointless. She'd known the Callahan family included some dangerous guys—everybody knew that. It hadn't scared her. Thanks to her mom's series of hard-living boy-friends, she knew how to look after herself.

Obviously, Patrick hadn't thought so. They were going to talk about that, and she was going to tell him exactly what she thought.

But not right now. Today was all about the pa-rade.

When Patrick had called, his father had jumped on the opportunity to help with the float, just as Torey had suspected he would. He'd shown up in record time, toolbox in hand, beaming from ear to ear.

"Just show me what you need done," he'd said. He'd worked steadily alongside Patrick until all the moving parts of the float had been running like silk.

"I could come by tomorrow," he'd offered, looking bashful. "Something might break at the last minute. I wouldn't mind standing by, just in case you need help with anything."

Patrick had glanced at his father, then at Torey. "Sure, if you don't have anything better to do. Be at the football field around one o'clock."

Simple words, but Ron's face had lit up as if he'd been handed a million dollars. Patrick still looked cautious, but he was letting Ron help—

even allowing him to take the lead—and Torey took that as a good sign.

*Please, Lord, let this work out,* Torey prayed. *Let these two be a family again.*

"Miss Torey, my leaves keep falling off!" Jill, dressed as a yellow chrysanthemum, tugged at Torey's sweater, holding up a handful of felt leaves.

"No worries, kiddo. We brought a sewing kit just for emergencies like this. Come over to the float and we'll get those back on in no time."

She was halfway through reattaching a leaf on Jill's sleeve when she heard the diesel engine roar to life. The Hope Center kids and volunteers broke into cheers and claps. Ron slammed the truck's hood closed and beamed at them.

"Good to go now!" he announced proudly.

"Miss Torey?" Josh appeared at her elbow, leading Lexie on her leash.

"Don't talk to her now, Joshie! She'll stick me with the needle," Jill ordered nervously.

"I'm not going to stick you. Just stay still. What is it, Josh?" Torey kept her eyes on her task. The stitches were huge and uneven, but she was in a hurry. They only had a few minutes before the parade was supposed to start, and the Hope Center's float was fourth in the lineup. Not much time to finish getting ready.

"I want to walk Lexie in the parade, but it's a

ong way. I got the wagon, so I can pull her in it
f she gets tired. But what if she gets thirsty?"

"There." Torey gave the last leaf an experimen-
al tug. "That should stay put. But don't you show
hose stitches to Mrs. Ruby or Mrs. Charlotte, or
'll be in big trouble."

"I won't! Thanks, Miss Torey! How come
ou're not dressed up, too?"

"I'm a little too big to be a flower," Torey
aughed.

"Paddy's dressed up as a farmer. You could be
he farmer's wife."

Torey's heart thrummed oddly at the idea, but
he shook her head. "Mrs. Ruby's going to be the
;ardener, remember? She'll ride on the float with
ou all, sitting in her rocking chair. I'm going to
»e in the crowd taking lots of pictures."

"Will you try to get one with me in it?" Jill
.sked shyly. "Some of the other girls' mamas are
aking their pictures, but I don't got a mama to
lo that."

"I sure will."

Jill gave her a quick hug then dashed off to
oin the bevy of flowers who would be riding on
he float.

"Miss Torey?" Josh repeated urgently. "What
f Lexie gets thirsty?"

"Here." Torey snagged a water bottle from the
:ooler she'd brought and grabbed a plastic cup.

"Stash these in your wagon. If Lexie gets thirsty, pour some water in the cup for her. Okay?"

"Thanks!" Josh accepted the supplies and led Lexie away. Torey smiled. A large poster was attached to the side of the boy's wagon proclaiming in crooked letters, "Everybody Needs a Friend! Adopt a Dog Today!"

She glanced back at the girls in their flower costumes. Jill and several other girls were standing awkwardly to the side as mothers positioned their daughters for photos. Torey frowned and glanced at Patrick, but he was wiping his hands on a rag and talking to his father.

Torey firmed up her mouth. She strode toward the women, pulling her phone out of her back pocket.

"Okay, flowers! Group pic!" she announced with an air of authority. The little girls crowded together, smiling, and she took several photos. "These are going on our Wall of Hope back at the center," she told them. "You girls look gorgeous." They grinned at her.

After several photos, she made a show of checking her watch. "Almost time," she said. "Anybody who needs to go to the restroom, better scoot over now. Jill, wait a minute."

Jill had started to go with the group, but she stopped, looking worried. "Am I in trouble?"

"Nope! I just want to get a few pictures of you

y yourself. Just for us. Okay? I'll take more dur-
ng the parade, too."

A smile broke over Jill's face. "Okay," she
greed happily.

Torey snapped several pictures—which wasn't
o easy since her eyes kept blurring. Silly, she
old herself, to get all teary-eyed. A five-year-
·ld beaming in a flower costume was nothing
o cry about.

"I think we have enough," she started, but a
oice spoke behind her.

"Just one more." Patrick spoke from behind
er. "Just a sec," he muttered, fumbling with this
hone.

"I better go to the bathroom, Paddy," Jill warned.

"Got it!" Patrick pressed a button.

"I'll go with her." Ruby walked up, a straw hat
lamped over her gray hair. "Wouldn't be a bad
Jea for me to visit the facilities before this gets
tarted. Come on, honey."

"Thanks, Ruby," Patrick said. "Josh? Come over
vith Lexie. I want to get some pictures of you, too."

Josh looked surprised. "Why? I ain't dressed
·p."

Patrick laughed. "You don't need to be for me
o want a picture of you. Stand right there. And
mile."

Josh let out a dramatic sigh, but he straightened
·is shoulders and grinned. "Be sure to get all of
.exie, okay? Not just her head."

"I will."

"You can take my picture, too, Miss Torey. mean, if you want to."

"Thanks, Josh. I was just about to ask." She took several shots, which she could only hope were good. Her eyes were blurring again.

"Attention!" The speaker system crackled to life. "Everybody should take their positions. We're about to get started."

"I hope the dog behaves herself," Patrick murmured. "I'm worried that the crowd might spook her. I'd feel better if one of us was walking with him, but I've got to drive."

*One of us.* Torey's heart dipped. "I could—"

"You can walk with the boy, son." Ron stopped beside them, looking hopeful. "I'll drive the truck."

"Oh." Patrick looked startled. "Thanks, but don't know—"

"Why not? I got my faults, but, Patrick, you know I can drive."

That was true. Ron's expertise with vehicles— like Patrick's—made him an expert driver. Torey held her breath, wondering what Patrick would say.

"I'm sure it doesn't matter who drives, as long as they hold a license," she pointed out. "And it might mean a lot to Josh to have you walking with him and Lexie. Especially if there did happen to be some problem he needed help with."

That seemed to make the decision.

"All right," Patrick agreed. "But go slow, Dad. And keep a check on your rearview to make sure everybody on the float is okay. And—"

"I've driven floats in parades before, son. I got this. Give me the keys."

Patrick handed them over. "Go get settled, Dad. They'll be starting this thing up in a minute. I need a quick word with Torey."

Ron hurried toward the truck. Patrick led her away from the crowd, heading for the chilly shade under the bleachers.

The familiar smell of dirt, popcorn, and metal hit her nose, coupled with the noise of a crowd. The combination reminded Torey of high school, when Patrick had played football. She'd come to the games, and more than once, he'd tugged her here to steal a quick kiss.

Her cheeks started to sting, and she pushed the memory away. "So?" she said lightly. "What did you need to talk about?"

"I saw what you did." He spoke with an intensity that made concern curl in her stomach. What was he talking about?

"I don't—"

"Jill was being left out of the picture taking. You fixed it."

"Oh, that." Torey was relieved. "She asked me to make sure I got a picture of her riding on the float, but I thought it'd be a good idea to take a few now, too."

"You made her feel special. I should have thought about that myself, but I didn't." He shook his head, looking frustrated. "I appreciate you stepping in. I saw you helping her with her costume, too. And giving Josh water, and... I just wanted to say thanks, Torey."

"Well, you're welcome. But honestly, it was nothing."

"It was something to Jill. And to Josh. And I—" He paused and looked away, over her shoulder through the slats of the bleachers at the floats lined up in the parking lot. The first song of the high school's marching band started with a loud, wobbly tuba blast.

It made them both jump—and laugh, as sweet memories crowded even closer. Patrick looked down into her eyes, and gently touched her cheek.

"It wasn't nothing," he said.

Then he leaned closer and covered her lips with his own.

# *Chapter Eleven*

His kiss felt warm and strong and familiar, and it drove every rational thought right out of her head. Her mind went to a blank screen, and nothing mattered—not the past, not the future, nothing except for this moment.

When he drew back and the cool autumn air hit her lips, she shivered. She opened her eyes to find him looking as surprised as she felt herself.

"Torey," he said. "I—"

"Paddy!" Jill called from the float. "Where are you?"

"Coming!" Patrick shouted over his shoulder. He turned back to Torey. "Listen. We—"

"Come quick! They're starting!"

The expression on Patrick's face was comical. She took pity on him.

"Go." She made a shooing gesture.

"But—"

"Later. We'll talk later. Now go before the parade starts without you."

"Later," he repeated, giving her one last, long look. Then he jogged to the float, which was rolling toward the road.

Feeling stunned, Torey followed the last of the crowd down the sidewalk to take her place on the parade route. As she turned to cut across to Main Street, she stumbled on the curb.

An older man caught her arm. "Better watch your step, Miss."

Torey blinked at him. "Thanks," she said.

"You're welcome." The man beamed at her. "Beautiful day for a parade, isn't it?"

Torey looked around. "Yes," she agreed. "Yes, it's a beautiful day."

The town of Cedar Ridge sparkled with joyful excitement. Businesses were decked out with hay bales, scarecrows, and other fall items, and many stores sported Closed signs as their owners stepped out to watch the parade.

The street was lined with people of all ages, everyone smiling, toddlers being hoisted on shoulders for a better view. The sidewalks were full, but not uncomfortably crowded.

It would have been different in Atlanta, Torey thought. Anytime there was an event there, the streets quickly became packed. She wasn't a fan of crowds, so she tended to hide away in her apartment whenever there were parades or other activities going on.

But this…this wasn't so bad.

She'd hoped to get an unobstructed look at the float and snap a few decent photographs, but most of the best spots were already claimed. She found some space behind a couple with two small kids. She wouldn't be able to get a great picture, which was a shame, but she'd be able to see the float if she stood behind the children.

She hadn't been there long before the woman noticed her. "Honey," she said to her husband, "Squeeze over and let this lady get in front so she can see."

"Oh, no," Torey protested. "That's okay."

"Don't be silly. Don's six foot three. He can see over your head just fine."

"Sure thing." Her husband motioned. "Come on up here."

"Well, thanks." Torey accepted the spot with a grateful smile.

There was a happy buzz of conversation in the crowd, and a ripple of applause as the Cedar Ridge High School marching band appeared. Resplendent in black and gold uniforms, the students advanced down the road, playing a shaky version of the school's anthem.

Torey smiled at the teenagers' earnest expressions and gasped with the crowd as the majorettes tossed their batons, catching them behind their backs. Just as the band marched past her, they tossed the batons again, but this time one girl missed her catch.

There was a collective moan of sympathy. Four people scooted forward, and the quickest one grabbed the fallen baton. She ran alongside the band to return it to its owner, who accepted it with an embarrassed smile.

"Don't you worry about that, honey!" called a woman in the crowd. "You're doing great!"

"Shake it off! Y'all are awesome!" called somebody else.

The deafeningly loud music reached another crescendo as the horns passed in front of her, and Torey saw the batons go shimmering up into the air again. The majorettes were too far down the street for her to see, but the struggling teenager must have caught hers this time. A round of cheers rose from the crowd.

"Atta girl!" somebody shouted.

"Look! Here comes the insurance company's float. They always have a real good one," a woman close to Torey exclaimed. A collective *oooh* went up from everyone but Torey.

She couldn't make a sound. The lump in her throat had gotten too big.

She couldn't remember the last time she'd felt so…happy. Maybe it was the friendly crowd, enthusiastically applauding a slightly off-the-beat band and a float consisting of wagon full of hay with a family dressed up as scarecrows waving at the crowd. Or the kindness of the man who'd steadied her arm, and of the family who'd nudged her up front.

Or maybe it was sweetness of a place with enough room to breathe, full of people who shouted encouragements to teenagers who dropped their batons.

The kind of place where you were kissed under the bleachers by a man with steady, sea-blue eyes who smelled of oranges.

Her heart stuttered at the memory.

The hay wagon and scarecrows were followed by a convertible with the mayor and his wife waving to the crowd, who politely waved back. Torey waved, too, but she wasn't really paying attention. Her mind kept darting from that heart-stopping moment under the bleachers to the future, when she and Patrick would talk about—

Everything they needed to talk about. That list was getting long.

Another collective intake of breath from the crowd was followed by loud applause.

"Look! Look!"

"Oh, that's precious!"

"That's gonna win the prize for sure!"

The Hope Center's float puttered up the street, its green crepe paper fringe rippling in the breeze. The children, whose costumes looked both homemade and absolutely adorable, waved happily from the float. Ruby, her straw hat mashed firmly down on her head, rocked in her rocking chair, holding a shovel upright like a scepter. A small girl dressed as a white and yellow daisy was seated on her lap. There were telltale tearstains on her face, but she must have recovered from her bout of stage fright, because safe on Ruby's knees, she was beaming at the crowd and fluttering her tiny hand.

Torey snapped pictures as older children, dressed like scarecrows walked along the edges of the road, handing out candy from their tin buckets. There was an approving murmur from the onlookers.

"Now, isn't that nice!"

"Say thank you to the cute scarecrow, Robbie!"

"That Hope Center's a real blessing. Does a lot of good in this town."

Torey's smile stretched so big her cheeks ached. She waved furiously at the children, who spotted her and pointed her out to each other.

She could dimly hear their voices over the crowd. *Miss Torey! Look, right there. It's Miss Torey!*

The kind mom leaned close and shouted, "Are they waving at you, honey? Do you know those kids?"

'Yes." Torey nodded. "I'm a director at the center," she explained.

"Oh!" The woman gave her a smile and a thumbs-up.

*Temporarily,* Torey started to add, but then she didn't.

She didn't want this job to be temporary. And she didn't want to move back to Atlanta.

She wanted to stay here in Cedar Ridge. With Patrick.

She glanced up as the float passed where she was standing and found Ruby looking down at her. As if the older woman had read her mind, her foster mom winked.

The little boy next to her bounced up and down. "Look at the doggie, Daddy!"

Josh and Lexie marched past, Josh handing out cards as swiftly as he could. Lexie strutted in front of him, her ears up and her tail wagging. Josh flashed Torey a hurried smile as he passed, but he turned his attention to the man next to her.

"Adopt a dog and make a difference," he said, handing out a card. He worked his way down the crowd, handing out the cards and repeating his words over and over.

"I'll take one of those cards," she heard a voice say.

"Me, too. I've been meaning to get a dog."

"Can I have an extra one? My mom's a widow, and she'd love a pup."

Josh politely handed out cards to all who asked—and some who didn't.

"He's doing great!" Patrick paused beside her, looking elated.

"He sure is! And so is Lexie."

"He's going to run out of cards at this rate," Patrick said.

Torey laughed. "That's okay. We made more cards than the shelter had dogs." The Hope Center float rumbled past, followed by a float sponsored by one of the local churches. "Better get going," she told Patrick. "You're going to be left behind."

"Right." He offered her a long, slow smile that made her knees go weak. "Later," he reminded her. He took four steps after the float, then stopped. He turned around and held out his hand.

"Come with me."

"But I'm not dressed up."

"You look fine." He wiggled his fingers.

"Aww," the mom murmured. "Go on, honey."

Torey took Patrick's hand. His fingers twined through hers, as strong and as warm and as comforting as his kiss had been. He gave her a tug.

"Better get moving," he said. "We're about to be flattened by Fellowship Community Church."

She laughed and hopped off the curb. As they walked hand in hand down the road, her heart pounded in time with their steps.

"Patrick? What exactly are we doing?"

He looked down and grinned. "I have no idea. We'll figure it out."

"Later."

"Later," he agreed, squeezing her hand.

Halfway down the route she saw her foster brother Ryder standing with his wife Elise and their twins. Logan, another foster brother, stood beside the curb in his sheriff's uniform, keeping a watchful eye on the proceedings from behind reflective sunglasses.

Elise waved at her, smiling. Torey waved back, and Elise elbowed her husband and pointed.

Ryder's jaw went slack with astonishment. He poked Logan, who turned his head in Torey's direction and slid his sunglasses down his nose.

Her brothers' eyes went from Patrick to Torey and then to each other. When they looked back at her with lifted eyebrows, she sighed. She had some explaining to do.

Patrick released her hand. She looked up to find his jaw set.

"Sorry," he muttered. "I've put you in a weird position. I should have thought…"

Torey reclaimed his hand. "Don't worry about it."

"Are you sure?"

She wasn't sure of anything right now, so instead of answering she just smiled.

A motion to the side caught her eye. Barton Myers had pushed his way to the front of the crowd. He was talking in Logan's ear, gesturing toward the Hope Center float.

As she watched, her brother's expression

shifted. He gave Barton a curt nod and strode out into the road in their direction, beckoning them to the side.

"Logan—" Torey started, but he ignored her, zeroing in on Patrick.

"I know you need to keep up with the kids, so I'll make this quick. Who's driving that truck?"

"My father," Patrick said, frowning. "Why?"

"He the one signed up on the form to do the driving?"

"No. He stepped in at the last minute."

"He been helping you out at the Hope Center?"

"Just last night and this morning, to get the float ready. Why? Is there a problem?"

Logan glanced back at Barton, who was watching them, his eyes narrowed.

The sheriff drew in a tired breath. "There might be. We'll meet up at the end of the parade route, and I'll fill you in."

Patrick strode along the road, trying to catch up with the Hope Center float, but his mind wasn't on the parade—or even Torey. It was on his father.

He couldn't believe this. What had his dad done?

Something bad enough that Sheriff Logan Carter had that *dealing-with-a-Callahan* look on his face. Patrick had spent years making sure law enforcement never looked at him like that again.

But less than twenty-four hours after he let his dad back into his life, here he was.

"Patrick."

Torey was having to jog to keep up with him. He slowed his pace. "Sorry."

At some point, he couldn't remember exactly when, they'd stopped holding hands. Who had let go first? He wasn't sure.

His heart panged, but he clenched his jaw. Probably just as well.

"I wasn't asking you to slow down," she said. "But calming down might be a good idea. You don't know what's going on yet."

"I can make a pretty good guess. Probably a bench warrant. A parole violation, maybe." Another idea occurred to him. "Or a suspended license. I didn't even check that."

"It may not be anything serious, Patrick. You saw who was doing the fussing. You know what a loose cannon Barton is about anything concerning the Hope Center."

"That's exactly why I shouldn't have let my father anywhere near the place. And with my family, where there's smoke there's not just fire. There's an inferno."

The parade had circled back to the football field. The marching band students scattered, the straight lines of their ranks falling apart. His dad pulled the truck into the parking lot, inching the float carefully past pedestrians.

"Let's get the kids squared away first," Torey said. "Okay? They need to be accounted for and all picked up, and—"

"I won't fight with my father in front of the kids, Torey," Patrick said impatiently. "I've been in this situation before, more times than I can count. I know how to handle it."

And he did. But the fact that he was having to handle it—again, after all these years—was rubbing his nerves raw.

Leaving Torey in his wake, he strode to the parked float. "Everybody on the float stay where you are. I'll pull out the ramps on the back so you can get down safely. Especially you, Ruby. Stay put until I can help you, all right?"

"Take your time." Ruby gave the little daisy-girl on her lap a final hug before setting her down. "I'm in no hurry."

Patrick and Torey rounded up the excited kids, gave praise, and listened to endless stories about the parade. One by one they were collected by parents and foster parents. When only Josh and Jill were left, Patrick went to help Ruby down. She studied the expression on his face, and her smile faded.

"Uh-oh. What happened?"

"Nothing yet," Torey answered before he could. "Logan just wants to talk to us. I think Barton's come up with something new to fuss about."

"That so?" Ruby leaned on Patrick's arm as he

led her down the ramps on the back of the trailer. "Any idea what?"

"Seems to have something to do with my dad."

Patrick's father was rounding the side of the truck, keys in his hand, his face creased with a smile. He stopped short.

"Me? What'd I do?"

"You tell me." Patrick closed the gap between them and took the keys out of his father's hand. "Logan Carter's headed this way, wanting to talk to us about you. Any idea why?"

"The sheriff?" Alarm sparked in his dad's eyes. "No, son, I got no idea. I've kept my nose clean since I got out."

"Have you been in touch with the rest of the family?"

"No, not really. I mean, a phone call or two, but—"

"You know how they are. You should've kept clear of them."

"I have been! I can't help who calls me on the phone, can I?"

"Give me your license." The sheriff's car was pulling into the parking lot. If he was going to figure out what was going on before Logan caught up with them, his time was limited. "I want to see if it's valid."

"It is!"

"I still want to see it."

"Patrick—" Torey's voice was pained.

"That's all right, Torey-my-Glory." Ron dug in his pants pocket for his billfold. "I got nothing to hide."

Patrick squashed his guilty feelings and flipped open the wallet to scan his father's license. It was current.

"Whatever it is, it's not that," he said, handing it back. Logan walked toward them, and Andy Marlow, the Cedar Ridge police chief, crossed the parking lot to join him.

Patrick's heart sank. Two officers, county and city—this couldn't be good.

"Officers," he said politely.

"Patrick," Logan answered in a level voice. He threw a cautious look at his foster mom. "Torey, you'd better take Ruby home."

"That's a good idea." Patrick wasn't sure what was going on, but anything involving his family was likely to be unpleasant.

And humiliating.

"I'm staying put," Ruby retorted. "This has something to do with the Hope Center. That's so, isn't it?"

Logan never flinched from telling the truth. "That's so."

"Then since I'm head of the board, it's my problem, too."

Logan didn't look pleased, but he didn't waste time arguing. He turned back to Patrick. "Then I'll get right to it. We need to clarify a few things."

"What's the trouble, Sheriff?" Ron's face had gone a few shades paler. "I hear it's something to do with me?"

"Yes, Mr. Callahan, I'm afraid it does," Logan answered. "There's been a child welfare complaint."

"A what?" Horror made Patrick's blood chill.

"A very general one," the police chief explained quickly. "A resident on the street where the Hope Center is located—"

"We know it's Barton," Ruby cut in. "No point beating around the bush."

Chief Marlow cleared his throat. "Anyhow, this citizen—"

"Barton—" Ruby inserted stubbornly.

"Has alleged that a convicted felon has been seen on the property interacting with the children, and he's concerned. Children's safety is something we take very seriously. We'd like to ask Mr. Callahan to come into my office and answer a few questions."

"I ain't done a thing wrong," Ron protested indignantly. "I was just helping with the float."

"We're not claiming you did anything wrong," Logan pointed out calmly. "But when a citizen—"

"Barton," Ruby interjected, more sharply.

"When *any* citizen," Logan continued, shooting his foster mom an exasperated look, "makes a complaint like this, we look into it. If there's nothing to it, this shouldn't take long."

"There ain't," Ron said. "And you can ask me whatever you want. You got to take me in the back of one of those patrol cars, or can I come in on my own?"

"I'll drive him," Patrick said. "I'd like to sit in on the interview, if that's allowed." He wanted to know exactly what was said, firsthand.

The two officers exchanged a glance.

"I don't see why that would be a problem." Logan's tone was civil but cool.

"Torey and I'll take Josh and Jill to my house," Ruby announced. "Likely this won't take any time to straighten out, and you can come pick them up after. That suit you?"

Patrick looked across the parking lot. Josh and Jill had climbed on the float and were playing with Lexie in the middle of a fake garden that was already looking a little ragged. And half the lights on the particle board barn were out.

That seemed appropriate. Everything beautiful he tried to make fell apart.

"Sure, Ruby. Thanks."

She leaned forward, gripping his arm with surprisingly strong fingers. "It's gonna be all right, Patrick," she whispered. "Things always look the worst just before the tide turns. That's the time to trust the Lord and hang on with all your might." She raised her voice. "Let's go kids. You're coming to my house for a while. We'll introduce that dog of yours to my goats!" She walked toward the float.

Jill clapped her hands and squealed, but Josh looked across at Patrick, his expression suddenly alert. Patrick made himself smile.

"I'll pick you guys up in a little while," he called.

"You're not fooling him," Torey murmured.

"No," Logan agreed. "He's seen too much trouble in his life for that." His eyes met Patrick's, and for the first time in years there was a glimmer of the old warmth there. "Be honest with him, Pat. No matter what. That's how he'll learn he can trust you."

"That's the plan."

Logan studied him for a second longer, then he nodded. "Good." He glanced at Torey, then back at Patrick. "If you want me to sit in on this interview, I can. It's a city thing, so technically not my jurisdiction, but if Andy doesn't mind—"

"I don't," the police chief said.

"I'll be happy to, if it'll make you feel more comfortable. Up to you."

It took Patrick a minute to answer. He understood what this gesture meant. If Torey was okay with Patrick, Logan was ready to mend fences.

"Yeah," he managed finally. "Thanks. I'd appreciate that."

"No problem," Logan said. "I'm sure this won't take long."

But as Patrick walked to his truck, he wasn't so sure. Josh wasn't the only one who could smell trouble coming. And right now, Patrick had a feeling that a lot of beautiful things were about to start falling apart.

# Chapter Twelve

Torey stood at the farmhouse window, watching the road. Then she glanced at her watch. Past seven, and there was no sign of Patrick yet.

"Sit down, child." Ruby came into the living room. Following her own advice, she dropped into her favorite armchair with a sigh. "You're not going to make him get here any faster by standing at the window."

"This wasn't supposed to take long," Torey pointed out irritably. "I wonder what's keeping him."

"Don't borrow trouble. No sense getting upset until you got the facts. And even then—" Ruby gave a tired chuckle "—it ain't like it helps."

"Where are Josh and Jill?"

"Sound asleep on the spare room bed with that dog. They were both tuckered out, and once they got their stomachs filled up, they were out like lights. Well," Ruby amended. "Jill was. Not so sure about the boy. He might have been playing possum. I think he's worrying himself, wondering what's going on."

Torey could sympathize. She was, too. She turned back toward the window. It was quickly growing dark, but there was no twinkle of truck headlights. She sighed.

"You know," Ruby said, a different tone in her voice. "I ain't heard you mention that boss of yours lately. You been making arrangements about getting back up there to work?"

Torey stiffened. "Not yet."

"Shouldn't you be?"

"He gave me three months." Gave was actually too generous a term. Grudgingly allowed was more accurate. "That's not up until around Thanksgiving."

"Just because he gave you the time don't mean you have to take it. You been wanting that job for a long while and seems to me you've already started off on the wrong foot. I'm doing fine now, so no reason for you to stay on if you're needed in the city."

That should have been reassuring. It was a good thing—a wonderful thing—that Ruby was doing so well. But instead of feeling reassured, Torey only felt…antsy.

She didn't want to go back to Atlanta. At least she didn't think she did.

She explored the idea cautiously, like the way

Ruby tapped the top of a buttermilk pie to see if it had finished cooking. She didn't trust these new feelings—about Cedar Ridge, about her job.

About Patrick.

She didn't trust them, but they sure weren't going away. They were only getting stronger. She needed more time to figure everything out before making a decision.

"There's the center to consider, too," she reminded her foster mom with some relief. "I can't dump all that on Patrick's shoulders."

"Don't see why not. He's got a wide set of 'em, and he's shouldered heavier things in his time."

"What about all this trouble with Barton?"

Ruby made a dismissive noise. "Always going to be trouble with Barton. If it ain't this, it'll be something else. Besides, Patrick won't be handling it alone. We'll find a director by the first of the year, I'm sure. In the meantime, I can pitch in some again now—with Patrick's help," she added when Torey started to protest. "And all the others, too. You've got a good lineup of volunteers now. It's not a one-woman job anymore, and I want to do my share."

Torey tensed. Did she see headlights? Yes, she did. "Patrick's here." She started for the door.

"Figured he would be sooner or later," Ruby said reasonably. "You think about what I said. Call that boss of yours and let him know you'll be back at your desk soon."

Torey closed the door without answering. She waited on the porch, while Patrick parked the truck. She watched him get out and start toward the house, and she knew.

Whatever news Patrick was bringing, it wasn't good.

He made it to the steps before he noticed her. When he did, he stopped and looked at her for a silent second. Then he squared his shoulders as if readying himself for a blow.

She'd crossed her arms against the chill in the mountain air, and she dug her fingernails into her flesh, letting the little pain steady her. Then she lifted her chin.

"It's going to be all right, Patrick," she said. "Whatever it is. We'll get through it. Together."

He knew it wasn't true. Things weren't going to be all right, or at the very least, they weren't likely to work out the way he'd hoped. Over the past few hours, that had become all too clear.

But standing here in the peace of Ruby's mountain farm, hearing Torey say the words he wanted to believe—that he wished he could believe…

He almost did believe.

Almost, but not quite. And somehow that flicker of hope made things harder.

"We'd better go inside," he said. "I need to talk to you. Ruby, too, if she's up."

"I'm up," called a voice from inside the house. Ruby had always been a shameless eavesdropper when it suited her. "It's not even eight o'clock. I'm old, but I ain't *that* old yet. Come on in and let's hear the worst of it."

Patrick accepted Torey's offer of a cup of coffee. Not because he wanted it, but because the time it took her to fix it allowed him to gather his thoughts. When Torey pressed the warm mug into his hands, he was as ready as he'd ever be.

"So." He set the mug on the end table next to his chair. "Dad and I talked to the police, and they looked up his records, and all that. Everything checked out fine. He hasn't been in any trouble since he got out of jail, and he's been meeting with his parole officer like he's supposed to. They don't think he's any danger to the kids, so him helping out at the center isn't a problem as far as they're concerned."

"Oh!" Torey's dark eyes sparkled with relief, and she visibly relaxed. "Well, that's good news, isn't it?"

"As far as they're concerned." Ruby repeated his last words in a knowing tone. "So it's a problem in some other way, I reckon."

"Yeah." He ran one hand through his hair. He hated this. "Something being a legal problem is one thing. This isn't one. But—"

"But it could still turn into a great big stink," Ruby finished. "If somebody wants it to. And I'm guessing that somebody does. I knew Barton wouldn't let this lie. What's he threatening now?"

"He's not threatening. After they looked into Dad's stuff and asked us some questions, the police chief phoned Barton and told him he didn't have a leg to stand on."

"I imagine Barton was ready for that." Ruby shook her head. "He's a pain in the neck, but he's smart."

"He had a plan B. Apparently, he's friends with the man who runs the online newspaper the *Cedar Ridge Herald*, and the guy worked with him to write a piece about the Hope Center. You can imagine what kind of stuff it says. In fact, you don't have to imagine. You can read it. The minute Chief Marlow made it clear he wasn't taking any action against Dad or the Hope Center, Barton told him the piece would be published. And he promised it would include the local law enforcement's reluctance to protect the kids from criminals. He's hinting that Logan's talked them into looking the other way because Torey and Ruby are involved."

"That's ridiculous!" Torey jumped to her feet, her eyes blazing. "Logan would never do such a thing! You know him, Patrick. He's allergic to lies, and his professional code of conduct is absolutely flawless. He'd never—"

"Settle yourself," Ruby ordered calmly. "Patrick ain't the one you got to convince."

Torey scrabbled in her back pocket for her

phone and tapped it furiously. "This thing is up now?"

"Yeah." He braced for an explosion. Torey wasn't going to like what she was about to read. He sure hadn't.

But Torey didn't explode. Instead, she sank back into her chair, her face stricken.

"Oh, no," she murmured, scanning the text on her phone.

"It gets worse," Patrick said.

She looked up at him, her eyes wide. "How? How could it get worse? This is...this is awful, Patrick. I mean, we know it isn't true, and the wording is careful, so we can't legally insist that they take it down. But what he's insinuating... it's bad."

"He made it clear that he'd be emailing that article directly to all involved parties. Including..." Patrick had to stop and swallow. "Including the social workers involved in the children's care. Specifically, Josh and Jill's social workers."

"That little rat," Ruby murmured with a snort. "Playing dirty, but smart, like I said. Folks do love a juicy story. This will be the talk of Cedar Ridge by lunchtime tomorrow. Won't matter what the police say once the town gets hold of it."

"Patrick." Torey looked horrified. "Could this jeopardize your adoption process with Josh and Jill?"

He hated to answer. He didn't want it to be

true, but it was, and he might as well face it. "Yeah. That was…a little bit of a long shot, anyway. But this…" He shook his head slowly. "I can't see Mitzi or Mrs. Darnell overlooking this. Especially not if it blows up like Ruby says."

"Oh, it will," Ruby assured him grimly. "Not many folks'll see it tonight. But by tomorrow morning, it'll be all over town."

"If God doesn't mean for Josh and Jill to stay with me…" Patrick paused. That was another thing it was hard to say. "Then I'm going to pray He finds them another home where they can stay together. They…need each other." He swallowed and tried a smile. "And it had better be a house with room for a dog, too. Because I can't see Josh giving Lexie up. Of course, if he has to go to a group home—"

"The Lord ain't gonna do that," Ruby cut in briskly. "Or," she amended, "I don't think He will. God surprises us sometimes, but we can trust that whatever He does, it'll be for the best." She stood up. "Sounds like we all got plenty of praying to do tonight. Tomorrow, you go ahead and call over to the DFCS office and get an appointment to meet with Mitzi and Mrs. Darnell. You let me know when it is, and I'll be there with bells on."

"I'll come too," Torey offered quickly.

"Better leave this to Patrick and me," her foster

mom said. "You need to talk to that boss of yours and make arrangements to get back to Atlanta."

"You're going back?" Patrick felt like a bug who'd just bounced off a windshield—and then been run over.

"I—" Torey started, but Ruby interrupted her.

"Of course she is. High time, too. Now, Torey, come and help me pack up some of that soup we had so Patrick can take it home. He needs to eat a hot meal tonight and get his strength up for tomorrow. Patrick, you go wake up them young'uns so they can get home and sleep in their own beds."

It felt oddly comforting to have somebody taking charge and bossing him around. As he passed Ruby on his way to the hallway, he paused and gave her a grateful, one-armed hug.

She patted his shoulder. "It's going to be all right," she assured him. "Barton may have the newspaper, but we got the Lord. This ain't even a fair fight."

## Chapter Thirteen

"I told you not to come," Ruby fussed as Torey helped her out of the car at the DFCS office. "You ought to be home talking to that boss of yours."

"Give it up, Ruby. I'm here, and I'm not going anywhere."

She wasn't, either. She was determined to see this through.

Patrick had called at seven and told them that he'd reached out to Mitzi and asked for an emergency meeting first thing this morning. The social worker had agreed to see him at 8:00 a.m.

Patrick had sounded tired.

"Did you explain what you need to talk to her about?" Torey had asked him.

"No. I didn't want to get into it until we were sitting there in person," he'd said.

"Tell him to bring Josh and Jill along with him," Ruby had instructed from the stove where she was scrambling fresh eggs. "They can miss a morning's school, and the social workers may want to talk directly with them, given what all's being said in that article. Best to do that right off."

Torey had relayed the information to Patrick, and he'd agreed with a dullness in his voice that wrung her heart. She'd never heard him sound so defeated before.

His truck was already in the parking lot, so he and the kids must be inside. Ruby and Torey walked into the old brick office building, and Torey shivered.

This place still smelled the same. Coffee and antiseptic and nervous sweat. Not an odor she associated with happy memories. She had a childish yearning to reach for Ruby's hand.

Maybe Ruby knew, because the older woman put an arm around Torey's waist and gave a squeeze. Patrick and the kids were nowhere in sight, so Ruby approached the receptionist behind the window.

"We're here for the meeting with Patrick Callahan, Darla. They already back in the conference room?"

"They are, Mrs. Ruby. Go on back."

Ruby led the way down the hallway, padded by the same worn beige carpeting Torey remembered. They turned a corner and found Patrick standing in front of a viewing window, looking inside at the playroom.

The large room was used for supervised parental visits and play therapy sessions. Today, Josh and Jill were there with a young social worker Torey didn't recognize. While Jill played with a wooden dollhouse, Josh slumped in a corner, arms crossed in front of his chest. He looked bored, but one leg jiggled nervously.

Patrick studied the children, his face unreadable, and Torey sighed. If this turned out the way they feared, Patrick's heart would break.

He gave them a sideways glance, offering a pained, twisted smile as they joined him. "I got Jill's hair right today," he said. "Took me all these months, but I finally managed it."

Sure enough, the little girl was sporting two even pigtails. "It—it looks perfect." Torey's voice cracked.

"Oh, now. Enough of that. You two put your chins up." Ruby laid one hand on each of their shoulders. "I spent some extra time last night praying over this, and I felt the Lord's peace. This is gonna be all right."

Patrick drew in a long, slow breath. "I could use some of that peace if you've got any to spare."

"Plenty to go around, but first you'll have to stop fretting over things you ain't in charge of. Now ain't the time to start doubting the good Lord, Patrick. Have you done all you can do, best as you can, honest as you can, for Josh and Jill?"

"I think so. Yeah."

"And can God be trusted?"

"He can."

"Well, then." Ruby shrugged. "We can rest easy. Our job's to trust God and do what's right. We may not know how He'll work all this out, but however it goes, it'll be for the best."

"You're right. But I've got to accept that God's plan may not be what I'm hoping for."

Ruby's expression softened. "That's true. Sometimes it ain't what we hope for." She gave his arm a maternal swat. "Sometimes it's a whole lot better."

"Good morning." Mrs. Darnell hurried down the hallway, glancing at her watch. "Sorry I'm running late. Busy morning. I see the children are squared away, so let's get started. Mitzi's waiting in the conference room."

Sure enough, she was, and Torey noted the chill in the social worker's voice as she greeted them. Not good.

When they'd settled around the table, Patrick cleared his throat.

"I guess you're wondering why I asked to meet with you," he said. Quickly, he laid out the situation. Barton's constant complaints, his father's presence at the center and the parade.

Mitzi took notes furiously. "You said your father was no longer a part of your life. Not,' she added under her breath, "that I'm surprised about any of this."

Before Patrick could respond, Ruby answered

tartly. "Circumstances change, Mitzi. In any case, the trouble's not with Ron Callahan, who served his time for what he did and who hasn't been in any trouble since. It's with Barton Myers."

Mitzi and Mrs. Darnell exchanged a look. Mrs. Darnell cleared her throat.

"Well, we're very sorry that the Hope Center is under attack, of course. We appreciate the center very much, and it's been a positive resource for this office for many years. We've been excited to see it being rejuvenated with new leadership." She favored Patrick and Torey with a cautious smile. "But I'm afraid I fail to see how these issues faced by the center impact this office or your case, specifically. Unless," she added, "there's more you've not yet told us?"

"I'm afraid there is." Patrick's face was tense and pale. "There's an article in the *Cedar Ridge Herald* that's likely to get a good bit of attention. It doesn't put me or my dad or this office in a very flattering light."

Mrs. Darnell lifted an eyebrow. "The *Cedar Ridge Herald*. That's the online newspaper?"

Mitzi tapped on her laptop. "Here it is." She pushed the computer over so that Mrs. Darnell could read the screen.

Torey watched as the two women scanned the article, trying to read their expressions. *Please, Lord,* she prayed over and over. *Please.*

She didn't know exactly what she was asking

for. Just for God to do what Ruby always said He would do—work things for good.

Then Mrs. Darnell's lips twitched.

It was a small thing. Torey probably wouldn't even have noticed it if she hadn't been watching so closely.

Mrs. Darnell wasn't—she couldn't be—amused? Torey had read that article herself, and there was absolutely nothing funny about it.

Mitzi and Mrs. Darnell finished reading about the same time. They exchanged a look.

"Well," Mrs. Darnell said. "That was certainly… um…interesting. But again, I fail to see the relevance here."

Now it was Ruby, Torey, and Patrick's turn to exchange a look.

"I'm sorry," Torey said. "Could we—" She gestured toward the laptop.

Mrs. Darnell obligingly turned it around, and the three of them leaned forward to look at the screen.

"Oh, *my*," Ruby murmured.

She was the only one who spoke. Patrick and Torey were both stunned into silence.

The article boasted an unflattering picture of Barton Myers, caught in midchew at some social function. And the article—

It was all about him. About how he'd made forty-seven complaints to local authorities about the Hope Center. About how he'd done something similar where he'd lived before, racking up almost a hundred nuisance complaints. Then he'd sold his former house at a profit to somebody who turned it into apartments, something it seemed his former neighbors weren't happy about.

Then there was a paragraph about how he'd opposed the construction of the town's beloved dog park. And how he'd blocked the funding for the library's new computers, which had ultimately been purchased by private donations.

The whole thing was a laundry list of Barton Myers's pettiness. It wasn't particularly well written. It seemed clunky, as if somebody had simply copied and pasted paragraphs from different sources. The byline read "A concerned citizen."

Ruby was chuckling. "It's true what they say. What goes around, comes around."

"Torey." Patrick's voice was strained. "I don't think the editor of the paper posted that article. You didn't—"

"No." That stung, but there was no time for hurt feelings. She sent him a sharp look, hoping he'd understand what she was trying to get across without her having to spell it out.

She knew of only one other person in Cedar Ridge with the skills to do something like this.

Patrick's eyes widened.

"So, this wasn't the article you expected us to see?" Mrs. Darnell asked.

"No," Patrick admitted. "I'm sure Torey has that one saved on her phone or something. She'd better show it to you."

"Patrick," Torey protested, but he shook his head.

"We've opened this can of worms. We're going to see it through. Show them."

Torey brought the file up on her phone and handed it to Mrs. Darnell. The two workers put their heads together as they read. She knew when they hit the part mentioning them by name. Mitzi went two shades paler.

"This is awful," Mitzi stammered. "It'll be a public relations nightmare."

"It's certainly not pleasant reading," Mrs. Darnell agreed grimly. "The new article appears to be a very positive change for all of us. Yet none of you seem relieved."

"I'm relieved," Ruby said.

A little smile tilted Mrs. Darnell's lips. "Except you," she conceded. "Does anybody want to enlighten me?"

There was a brief silence, again broken by Ruby.

"Got to trust the Lord," she murmured, looking at nobody in particular. "Good book says the truth'll set you free."

Mitzi was studying them, her expression suspicious. It wouldn't be long before she put two and two together.

Torey watched Patrick struggle. Then he swallowed hard.

"We'd better bring Josh in here," he said.

"Yeah, I did it. And I ain't sorry." Josh stared at them defiantly, but Patrick noticed that the boy was shaking.

"You hacked into the newspaper's database and changed the original story to this one." Mrs. Darnell still appeared to be struggling to comprehend this. "*You* did this. By yourself. No adult helped you. Not, say, Torey here."

Torey flushed, but Josh shook his head.

"I didn't need no help. It was easy. Lots easier than hacking into the school's system. And that guy deserved it, saying all those mean things."

"I told you," Mitzi said, shaking her head.

"But where did you get this information? Did you make it all up?" Mrs. Darnell asked.

"No!" Josh said indignantly. "I ain't a liar. All that's true. I found it searching around the internet, and I just sorta put it all together."

"So, we can add plagiarism to hacking," Mitzi muttered.

"What's that mean?" Josh demanded.

"It means you can't pass other people's writing off as your own work," Mrs. Darnell explained.

"Oh. Like copying off somebody else's paper at school."

"Sort of."

"I didn't put my name on it. I wasn't trying to get credit or nothing. I just wanted people to know the truth so they wouldn't believe that guy no more."

"I think we can set that aside for now," Mrs. Darnell said. "Plagiarism appears to be the least of our problems."

Patrick felt bewildered—and miserable. No way was Mitzi letting the adoption go through after this. "Josh, we talked about this. You know hacking's wrong. You weren't even supposed to be using the computer. It was off-limits…" He trailed off.

"What that man was doing was wrong, too." For the first time, the boy's voice wobbled. "I'm sorry about using the computer when I wasn't s'posed to, but I didn't want everybody reading that other stuff. Mrs. Ruby said it would be all over town if it was still there in the morning. So, I changed it last night."

"Wait a minute," Torey said. "How'd you even know about the article, Josh? Or what Ruby said?"

"Wondered when somebody'd get around to that," Ruby spoke to the air.

"I heard you all talking. I got out of the bed and went down the hall and I heard…" His voice caught as he glared at the social workers. "I heard about how because of this man we was going to get moved out of Paddy's house probably. And how you wouldn't let him adopt us, and how we was probably going to be split up, all because of that Barton man." The boy swiped a hand roughly across his face. "I didn't even know we was going to be adopted. Nobody told me." He sounded indignant.

Patrick patted the empty chair beside him. "Sit down, son." When Josh had dropped into the seat, he went on, "I'm sorry you didn't know about that. I'd only talked to these ladies here a little while ago about it, and they had some paperwork and things to do. Things were just getting started."

"Your adoption by Mr. Callahan was only a possibility," Mitzi said. "We'd have discussed it with you and your sister if things had gone much farther."

Patrick's heart sank. She sounded as if the adoption was off the table. Which, he knew, it surely was. But that didn't make this any easier.

"This is my fault," he said. "I don't know much about computers, and I haven't been able to provide Josh with enough guidance. I was working on that...but—"

"He is," Torey supplied quickly. "He asked me to find a mentor for Josh, to help him manage his talent for technology."

"It's a little late for that," Mitzi said dryly, but Mrs. Darnell looked interested.

"And did you?"

"I did. If you let this adoption go forward, you

have my word that Josh's computer activities will be well supervised."

Who had Torey found? She hadn't mentioned anything like that to him. For a second, Patrick wondered if she was being completely honest, but from the look on her face, she was.

"I appreciate that," Mrs. Darnell said. "Because this is a very serious thing, Joshua. You do realize that, don't you? You're developing a pattern of misbehavior when it comes to computers that's very alarming."

"I've been good for a long time," Josh protested. "I'd of kept on being good if this hadn't happened."

"That's not the way it works," Patrick explained miserably. "We can't use what happens to us as an excuse to do something wrong."

"Mitzi?" Mrs. Darnell turned to the social worker. "You've worked closely with this case. What are your thoughts?"

Here it came. Patrick braced himself for the worst.

"Maybe Josh had better go rejoin his sister while we talk this over," Mitzi suggested.

"No!" Josh jumped to his feet, sending his chair skittering backward. "People are always talking behind our backs, making decisions about us. They never ask us nothing, and half the time we don't even know what's going on. When that other lady took us to Paddy's house, we didn't know we was going until she picked us up at school. Had our things in a trash bag in her trunk. She didn't bring Jill's favorite shirt 'cause it was in the laundry. If I'd known we was moving, I'd have got that shirt for her, but I didn't know. I never know. So, you tell me right now what you're gonna do."

"The boy's got a point," Patrick said. "He has a right to know."

Mrs. Darnell considered Josh thoughtfully. "Obviously you're a very smart young man," she said slowly. "So, I think I'll ask you a question. What do you think we should do?"

Josh's mouth trembled. Then the boy stuck his chest out and nodded toward Patrick.

"Let him adopt Jill. You can move me to that group place they was talking about if you want to. But let Jill stay with Paddy."

Patrick blinked. So, there it was. Josh didn't want to stay with him—so much, in fact that he was willing to be separated from Jill if that's what it took.

He hadn't expected that, and it knocked the wind right out of him. He'd really thought he was making progress with Josh.

"Why do you think this would be the best solution?" Mrs. Darnell was asking gently.

"Jill really likes him. And he's…," Josh swallowed. "He's good to us. He don't yell. And he fixes us supper every single night, even though he's not good at cooking. He's not so good at doing Jill's hair, either. Or he wasn't. But at night after we go to bed he watches videos on YouTube, and he gets better. He don't hardly know how to use computers, but he figured that much out just so he could help us.

"I see," Mrs. Darnell said.

"A fellow don't do stuff like that if he don't care. None of those other foster parents we had watched any videos. Our own mama and daddy didn't care enough to do that." Josh jerked his head in Patrick's direction. "But he does. I—" The boy's voice cracked. "I can't take good care of Jilly. I tried, but I'm… I'm just a kid. He can do it better than me. You should let him have her."

"Now, I don't think—" Mitzi started, but Mrs. Darnell shook her head.

"Not now, Mitzi. So, Josh," she went on. "You think we should allow Mr. Callahan here to adopt your sister, is that correct?"

Josh nodded.

"But not you?"

"No. Just Jill."

"Why not you?"

"'Cause I ain't no good. I keep messing up." He turned to Patrick, desperation in his eyes. "Jill's good and sweet and only little. If I go to that home, they'll let you keep her. And Lexie, too. You'll take care of Lexie, won't you? I don't s'pose they'll let me have a dog at that group place." He made it to the end of that sentence and then choked.

Patrick was on his feet in an instant, gathering the boy close. "You're not bad, Josh," he said in the child's ear. "You're not." He turned to the social workers. "You can't split these kids up. Look at this. Look at what you're doing to him. It's cruel, and it's wrong, and I'm not standing for it. If you try, the article Barton wrote won't be anything compared to what I'll put in the paper."

"And I'll help him write it." Torey was on her feet, too. "You have a perfectly good home right here for both of these children. There's no reason for you to pass it up."

"Please sit down," Mrs. Darnell said mildly.

"Not until you hear me out," Torey insisted. "These children deserve a father like Patrick Callahan. He's going to save their lives, if you'll get out of the way and let him. You want to know how I know that? This lady right here." Torey put her hand on Ruby's shoulder without taking her eyes off the two women across the table. "She saved my life, and I was a lot more trouble than Josh could ever hope to be."

"Miss Bryant, I appreciate your concern and your perspective, but technically you're not involved in this situation, so—"

"Yes, she is," Patrick said. Everybody looked at him, but he had no idea what to say next. "She's involved," he repeated.

Torey turned toward him, a stunned look in her eyes. She seemed to be asking a question. He wasn't sure what that question was, exactly. But he knew the answer.

He nodded firmly. *Yes*

"I'm involved." Torey's face lit up with a new warmth—and even more determination. She turned back toward the social workers. "And I guarantee you I'll get more involved if you take either of these children away from the only person who's ever truly cared about them."

"You're both wasting your breath." Ruby spoke from her chair, and all eyes swiveled to her, and Patrick's heart sank. "If you two hotheads would settle down, you'd likely hear that for yourselves. Go ahead." She nodded at Mrs. Darnell. "You ain't fooling me. You've already made up your mind. You'd better tell 'em. Ain't no point in dragging this out."

## Chapter Fourteen

"Ruby, stop bossing me around." Mrs. Darnell shook her head ruefully. "But you're right. I've made up my mind. I see no reason why your adoption process can't go forward, Mr. Callahan. For both the children."

Patrick's knees gave out, and he dropped back down on his chair with a thud. He kept one arm around Josh as he stared at the social worker.

"Mrs. Darnell, we should talk," Mitzi said. "I don't think this would be a suitable placement. If you'll review my reports—"

"Oh, we'll talk, Mitzi. I assure you." Something in the other woman's tone must have quelled her, because Mitzi closed her mouth with a snap. "And I've already reviewed your reports. They're very thorough, but they're missing some important elements." She waited a beat. "Optimism. Faith. Encouragement. I see no evidence of those in any of your assessments of Mr. Callahan—

or frankly, of most of your other cases. This is a difficult and often heartbreaking job, but we can't allow ourselves to become jaded. Our clients need us to expect their success and to help them move toward it."

"But surely," Mitzi began cautiously, "in this case—if you consider what this boy has done—"

"I am considering it, believe me. You should be considering it, too. He just offered to sacrifice his own future for the sake of his little sister. He also expressed a great willingness to entrust Jill to Mr. Callahan's care. What does that tell you?"

"I—" Mitzi looked uncertain, and Mrs. Darnell made an impatient noise.

"Trust is precious currency for our children, Mitzi. They don't spend it carelessly. Josh gave us a very clear, very concise explanation of why he's chosen to trust Mr. Callahan. Despite what your reports say, I believe this placement has been a resounding success, and I have no reason to believe that adoption wouldn't be the best thing for everybody concerned."

"Does—does that mean I ain't got to go to that group home?" Josh asked. "I can stay in Paddy's house with Jill?"

"That's exactly what it means, Josh. Now," she went on in a sterner tone, "this misconduct of yours where computers are concerned? That has to stop. Come along with me to my office, and we'll phone the editor so you can apologize and get this straightened out."

Josh looked unhappy. "But what if he puts that other article back up? The one that gets everybody in trouble?"

"After I speak to him, I don't think he will." There was a steeliness in Mrs. Darnell's voice that made Patrick smile. Suddenly he didn't think the editor would, either.

"Thank you," he said.

"You're welcome. Since Josh is still our responsibility, I'll take care of smoothing this over, but once he's legally your son, that becomes your job. I applaud your efforts to find him a mentor. Miss Bryant, given your involvement with this family am I to assume you might be taking on that role?"

"I—" Torey looked at Josh and Patrick. "I'm not sure."

"Well, you and Mr. Callahan can sort that out." She rose to her feet. "The sooner the better because we certainly don't want any more incidents like this one."

"That might be a problem," Ruby said. "Torey's got a real good job in Atlanta, and she's got to—"

"Ruby," Torey interrupted. "That doesn't matter. I'll find some way to help Josh. If, that is, Patrick wants me to. I'm sure we could…figure something out."

Patrick's heart thudded. "I hope so," he murmured.

Mrs. Darnell looked from one of them to the other, and that little tickle of a smile tipped up her lips again. "I see. Why don't you work out a few of the details? Privately. You can use Mitzi's office."

"My office? But—" Mitzi started to protest, then she subsided. "Sure," she said. "Go ahead. I can wait in here."

"Good," Mrs. Darnell said. "Now, come along, Josh. Let's get this over with."

When she'd ushered Josh out of the meeting room, Patrick turned to Torey. "We have some things to talk about," he ventured.

She nodded. "We sure do."

Ruby cleared her throat, and Patrick saw her shoot Torey a long, meaningful look. His heart fell.

He thought—he hoped—Torey had changed her mind about Cedar Ridge. Maybe about…a lot of things.

But going by that look, Ruby's mind hadn't changed. She still believed Torey belonged in Atlanta.

Not here, not with a guy like him.

And he wasn't completely sure she was wrong.

Torey looked at her foster mom. Her heart, which had bobbed upward with reckless hope, jerked back down like a balloon held by a grumpy toddler.

Time to get this settled. She turned to Patrick and Mitzi. "Could Ruby and I have the room for a moment?"

"Sure," Patrick said immediately. "I'll wait in Mitzi's office."

Mitzi huffed a sigh and glanced at her watch. "I'm going out for breakfast," she announced.

As Patrick left the room, his eyes sought Torey's. He looked worried. She met his gaze squarely.

"This won't take long," she promised.

As soon as the door had closed behind him, she turned to Ruby.

The older woman shook her head. "I got a feeling what you're going to say. You're a grown woman, and I ain't gonna tell you what to do. But remember—you got a whole life down in Atlanta waiting for you. One you bought and paid for with a whole lot of hard work. That's a lot to give up."

"It is," Torey said. Then she shrugged "And it isn't."

Ruby drew in a long breath. "You wasn't happy here before. What makes you think you'll be happy here now?"

A slow smile broke over Torey's face. "People can change, Ruby. I'm not sure what Patrick's going to say..."

"Oh, I got a pretty good idea," Ruby murmured.

"But if he does want me to…stay…"

"I'm a sight more interested in what you want. And you don't have to tell me what that is. It's written all over your face."

"So? Do I have your blessing?"

Her foster mom snorted. "You always got my blessing, child. You don't have to ask me for that."

"Then I'll ask you for something else." Torey steadied herself with a deep breath. "I want the job as director of the Hope Center. Full-time and permanently."

She expected Ruby to look shocked, but the older woman's hazel eyes regarded her calmly. "Won't make near so much money as you were making down in the city."

"I don't care."

"Fiddling with computers will only be a part of it. Lots of other things to see to."

"I'll manage. And—" her heart gave a funny little jump "—hopefully I'll have a lot of help."

"What if you don't? What if things with Patrick don't work out? Didn't before."

Torey's hopes sagged, but she squared her shoulders. "I'd still want the job."

"Why?"

"I can't explain it, Ruby. Only that I…come alive there. Helping the kids, trying to make their futures better…it matters to me. And I've got so many ideas of what we can do! I can write up a proposal for you, so you can see. I've already got some spreadsheets started about how to finance it, and—"

"I'll take your word for it," Ruby said. "So, you're sure and certain it's what you want?"

"I'm sure and certain."

"I'll talk to the rest of the board, then, but I think it's safe to say the job's yours."

"Thank you, Ruby!" Torey threw her arms around Ruby in a fierce embrace.

"You're welcome. Now, I reckon you'd better go settle up things with Patrick. He's gonna need to get those young 'uns back in school so they don't miss too many of their lessons. I'll be waiting here for you."

Somehow the quiet promise made Torey choke up. "You always have been, Ruby. Always waiting there for me. Even when I don't pay attention to your advice."

"And I always will be. Now, get. Mitzi's office is the third door on the left."

Torey gave Ruby one last squeeze, then left the conference room. She didn't have to count the doors. Patrick was standing in the doorway, waiting for her.

He drew her inside and closed the door. "We need to talk," he said.

"Yes, we do." A heavy smell of perfume hung in the air, and she wrinkled her nose.

"I'm stuck here, Torey. In Cedar Ridge. For a long time, anyway. I've got my business to run, and the house. And I can't move the kids, not while I'm still fostering. And even after I adopt them—"

"It would be tough on them to move. I get it. They're going to need consistency more than most kids."

"Yeah." Patrick nodded. There was a desperate but determined glint in his eyes. "And you... you've got that great job in Atlanta."

"Not anymore."

"You've got a whole life down there, and—" He stopped. "What?"

"I just asked Ruby for the job as the director of the Hope Center. The permanent director."

There was a long, incredulous pause. "You did?"

"I did."

"What did she say?"

Torey smiled. "She gave it to me."

He studied her, hope dawning on his face. "And you want to stay here? You really want to stay here? For good?"

She lifted one eyebrow. "I guess that depends. Was there anything else you wanted to talk to me about?"

"Yeah, there is." Patrick's smile faded, and he ran one hand through his hair. "I don't know how to do this. Last time I planned it all out, and it still went wrong." He looked at her. "I took you to the lake, remember? And I rented a boat."

Torey's heart was pounding so hard she couldn't think. "I remember. It had a leak."

"I wanted to kneel down because that's what guys did in the movies. But kneeling in a boat…"

Torey smiled. "It got wobbly."

"The knees of my pants got soaked because the thing was taking on water. And when I took the ring out of my pocket." He opened his hand, and a slim gold band with a petite diamond flashed in the light.

Torey's breath caught in her throat. "You still have it."

"Fished it out of the back of my drawer this morning. I've never met anybody else I wanted to give it to. You're a hard act to follow, Torey Bryant. Last time I was terrified I was going to drop the thing overboard, so I just jammed it on your finger without even asking you."

Last time. Her heart pounded harder, and she smiled.

"You didn't have to ask me. Not then. And not now. The answer was always going to be yes." She tiptoed up to kiss him, and he leaned down. At the last second he pulled away.

"Torey," he ground out, "it's not the same now as it was then. I have the kids."

"And a big, goofy dog," she reminded him.

"And there's my family." He paused. "I've set

boundaries with them, but I can't promise you they won't impact our life."

*Our life.* One life, shared. If her heart beat any faster, it was going to come right out of her chest. An intense joy radiated all the way to her fingertips.

"They might. On the other hand, if they're not careful, we might impact theirs."

"You're sure? I hope you're sure." He ran his hand through his hair again. "I know I can't... offer you much. But, Torey, if you think...if there's any way that you..." He broke off and shook his head. "I can't. I've messed this all up again. This is so...wrong."

Her heart fell. "What's wrong?"

"This." He gestured around the office. "Maybe the lake didn't turn out to be that great of a choice, what with the leaky boat and all, but this...this is way worse. I know the memories you have, Torey, of places like this. Of how rotten your life was before you went to Ruby's." He took a breath, and his eyes shifted to that darker blue that meant he was upset. "I know how people hurt you. This... should be happy, us making a start together. It should happen in a happy place, not here."

Her heart was acting like a yo-yo. It soared upward again, spinning joyfully. Torey looked around. The room looked exactly like all of the other social workers' offices she'd been in. And there'd been plenty of them.

A computer—adequate but not the latest model. Scuffed-up furniture and an overflowing trash can. Big gray filing cabinets and a teetering stack of color-coded files on the desk, all no doubt containing cases of children in tough situations. A desk calendar with endless scribbles on it, noting appointments, many of them crossed out with red ink because somebody hadn't shown up when they were supposed to. A chipped coffee mug with a Mitzi-colored lipstick smear next to a jumbo-sized bottle of aspirin.

Yes, she'd suffered in offices like this. In this very building, probably in this very office before Mitzi had inherited it. She'd been hurt, first by the deeply flawed parents who were supposed to love her and later by the imperfect system that was supposed to help her.

Then Ruby had whirled into her life like a gray-haired cyclone, stirring up the debris of her past and blowing it far enough away that it didn't bother her so much anymore.

And now here she was back in the same building, standing next to a man she loved beyond all reason, looking at a future that sparkled with hope and possibilities.

She put a hand on each side of his cheeks, tilting his face down toward her own.

"This," she whispered, "is the perfect place. Because you know what? This place and all its hurts are part of me. Your family's problems are part of you. Josh and Jill's pain is part of their stories, too. Maybe we don't like that, maybe the memories sting, but they made us who we are. We couldn't have the joy without the pain. I don't think you could have picked a better place for us to start over, Patrick Callahan. So, if you have something to ask me, go ahead."

His eyes were riveted on hers. "Marry me, Torey." It wasn't really a question. But then, of course, it didn't have to be.

She started to say yes. She meant to. But he must have read her answer in her eyes, because his face lit up with joy, and before she could speak, he covered her lips with his own.

# Epilogue

"So, this party is because Miss Torey's going to marry us?" Jill asked as Patrick pulled his truck to a stop in Ruby's yard a week later.

One wonderful, hard-to-believe week later.

"That's right," Patrick reassured her as Josh groaned.

"Jilly, give it a rest. You've asked him that forty-billion times already. He always says yes."

"Right," Jill nodded, making her picture-perfect pigtails bounce. "'Cause she *promised*. And Miss Torey doesn't break her promises. And you're both going to 'dopt us."

Josh groaned again, but Patrick laughed. "Yep."

"So, we're gonna have a daddy and a mama. Me and Josh both."

"Yep."

"Forever."

"Yep."

Patrick opened the truck door, careful not to

ding a Jeep he didn't recognize, one of many vehicles in the crowded yard. A rental, he realized after a glance at the tag. Probably Torey's foster brother Nick's. That's why Maggie and Ruby had put together this engagement party so fast. Nick, who was always off in some remote part of the world, had blown back into town for an undetermined amount of time.

His father's old Chevy was there, too. Patrick smiled, remembering how thrilled Ron had been at the invitation.

"I'll be there, son," his father had assured him. "With bells on."

He shepherded the kids toward Ruby's farmhouse. Torey must have been watching from the window because she met them on the porch.

"Hi!" She tousled Josh's hair and gave Jill a hug.

"Something smells good," Josh said, sniffing hopefully.

"You're in for a treat. Wait until you see the cake Maggie brought! And Uncle Nick's cooking up some kind of candy he learned how to make while he was in Portugal." Torey stopped and frowned. "Or maybe Brazil. I don't remember. Anyway, it looks delicious. Your cousins are helping him. You can, too, if you hurry."

"Come on, Joshie!" Jill ran into the house, tugging her brother along with her. A split second later, there was a loud cheer from inside, punctuated by Jill's delighted laughter.

"Wow," Patrick said. "Sounds like quite a welcome."

Torey snorted. "Wait until we walk in together. They're all going to act like idiots." She twined her arm around his waist, and he pulled her close, marveling how well they fit together.

"You sure you're ready for this?" she asked.

He smiled and leaned down to kiss the tip of her nose. "If you can deal with my family, I can deal with yours."

Although there was one of them he did feel a little nervous about facing. He hadn't spent much time with Ruby since he and Torey had emerged from Mitzi's office engaged. He couldn't imagine she was too pleased about Torey's decision to give up her job in Atlanta and marry him, but so far she hadn't said anything directly to him about it.

Knowing Ruby, though, he'd hear from her sooner or later.

Torey was right about their welcome. A deafening cheer greeted them when they walked into the kitchen arm in arm. Patrick was slapped on the back, fist-bumped, hugged, teased, and congratulated by one of Torey's siblings after another.

At one point, he found himself face-to-face with Logan. The sheriff looked at him for a solemn second. Then he grinned.

"Congratulations, *brother*." He gave Patrick a

fierce, hug, thumping him on the back so hard
that Patrick coughed. "Let's meet for lunch one
day this week, okay?"

"Count me in," Ryder ordered from the table
where he and his wife Elise were fixing plates
for his twin nephews.

"Me, too," Nick said. "I need all the family
time I can get while I'm in the country."

Family. He had a real family. He noticed his
dad leaning against Ruby's counter, well within
earshot.

"Sure. Dad, you want to come to lunch, too?"

"Me?" Ron looked astonished—and grateful. "Well, yeah. I mean, if the rest of 'em don't
mind."

Logan gave the older man one of his long, level
looks. "Nobody minds. You're part of our family, too, now."

It took Ron a minute to speak. "Thanks."

"That's settled, then." Logan scooped his step-
son Danny out of the way of the people placing
more food on the already crowded table.

A few times during the meal, he caught Ruby
looking in his direction, her faded hazel eyes
catching his, but she kept her distance. After supper, she motioned to Charlotte, who brought her
a large gift bag, decorated with wedding bells.
Ruby handed it to Torey with a smile.

"It's for you," she explained simply.

Torey settled the bag on her lap and dug under

the tissue paper. "Oh," she said, her hands stilling. "Patrick, look." She carefully pulled a quilt out of the bag.

He rose to help her unfold it. They held it up, one on each side, looking down at the design. Beautiful loops of multicolored fabric intertwined on a cream background.

"It's a double wedding ring pattern," Charlotte explained over the oohs and ahs. "Ruby picked it out."

There was something odd in her tone. Patrick frowned, puzzled, but Torey paid no attention. She was busy examining the quilt.

"These are from my old shirts," she said, her finger tracing one of the designs. "And look, Patrick. I think this is supposed to be for you." She pointed out a piece of fabric printed with vintage Chevrolets. And another one, with old-fashioned advertising signs. These were looped in with Torey's.

"Didn't have none of your old shirts to use, Patrick," Ruby said. "So, Charlotte helped me order them pieces. It turned out real pretty, don't you think?"

This was as good an opening as any. "It sure has. Ruby, could I—speak to you for a minute? Alone?"

"Surely." The older woman rose from the table. "We'll go out on the porch. Y'all go on and cut that cake before the little ones bust from waiting. We'll be right back."

Torey sent him a questioning look, and he squeezed her shoulder as he passed. He'd explain later.

He opened the front door, ushering Ruby outside. Night had fallen already—the days were growing shorter as the autumn aged. After the crowded warmth of the house, the air felt cold.

"So?" Ruby rubbed her arms. "Whatever you got to say, say it before we both catch a chill."

"I want to say I'm sorry, Ruby. Coming back here…marrying me…that's not what you wanted for Torey. I understand how hard making that quilt must have been for you. I wanted to tell you how much I appreciate it. And to promise you that I'm going to do everything I can—everything— to make Torey happy."

Ruby waited a second. "That all you got to say?"

"That—and that I hope you can forgive me."

"Oh, you children." Ruby sighed—then swatted his arm so hard that he flinched. "The trouble with you is that you don't listen. And you don't know near as much as you think you do."

Patrick rubbed his arm. The little woman packed a punch. "What are you talking about?"

She smiled, her eyes twinkling in the dim light. "I never said I didn't want Torey to move here. I just said she'd lose her job if she didn't go back to Atlanta, which was the truth. And I asked you to try to get her to move back there because I thought it would be helpful. I remember exactly what I said, 'cause I picked my words careful. I'm a faithful Christian woman, and I don't hold with lying. But," she went on, "sometimes when folks are extra stubborn, you got to get a little... creative."

Patrick frowned. "Do me a favor and spell this out for me, Ruby."

"All right. I will. How long do you think it takes to make a quilt like that one, son? A sight longer than a week, I'll tell you that much."

"*Ruby.*"

She cackled. "Smarter than I look, ain't I? And not a bad little matchmaker neither."

He was having some trouble wrapping his mind around this. "Are you saying this—all of this with Torey and me—was your doing?"

"Oh, no. It's the Lord's doing. I just helped Him along a little." She arched an eyebrow. "Are you complaining?"

"No." A smile broke over his face. "I feel a little blindsided, but no, I definitely am not complaining."

"Smart man. And if you're serious about gettin' in my good graces, you can calm Torey down once she figures this out. That'll happen about any minute now."

"What'll happen any minute?" Torey stepped out onto the porch. "Sorry, but I thought Ruby might need a sweater."

"No worries. We're all done. Now, you two can stay out here as long as you want. Me, I'm going back to the kitchen and warm up with some coffee and cake."

Torey closed the door behind her foster mom and walked toward Patrick. "Everything okay?"

He looked down into her dark eyes, sparkling with starlight—and love. He smiled.

"Everything's perfect."

"You know, it is." Torey sounded as if she couldn't quite believe it. "Absolutely perfect. I was afraid Ruby wouldn't be as excited about this as everybody else. She was so worried about me giving up that Atlanta job. But now we know she's all right with it because she's made us a quilt. That's a ton of work, not to mention her special ordering the material for your part and— wait a minute." Torey frowned. "Patrick! A quilt like that takes a month at least. How did she—"

He grinned, watching Torey work it out. "Ruby just reminded me that she's smarter than she looks. Apparently, she's smarter than both of us put together."

"That old rascal played us, Patrick. She was matchmaking the whole time. She even hinted that she was going to do it. *Whatever somebody tells you to do, you're bound and determined to do the opposite.*" Torey shook her head. "I can't believe it. This is just—"

He put his arm around her and snugged her in close. "Perfect," he reminded her.

She looked up at him. Another burst of laughter swelled from the farmhouse behind them, and he could hear his father's rich, rolling chuckle mixed in with the rest. As he watched, the indignation sparkling in Torey's eyes shifted into something sweeter.

"Absolutely perfect," she agreed. As she tiptoed to kiss him, the chill of the mountain air gave way to the warmth of family, forgiveness, and love.

\* \* \* \* \*

Dear Reader,

Thanks so much for coming along on this fourth trip to Cedar Ridge, Georgia! I'm excited to be visiting this sweet little mountain town with you!

You know what makes a place special to me? The people! I may admire the scenery and appreciate the food, but it's the people who will bring me back time after time—in a story or in real life.

Patrick and Torey were such interesting characters! I loved how Patrick evolved as a foster parent, pushing past his own sense of inadequacy to meet the needs of the kids in his care. Torey was fun, too, as she navigated the unexpected turn her life had taken in this story—and as she discovered that her stubbornness was no match for Ruby's matchmaking skills!

I've enjoyed writing all these stories about Ruby and her foster kids because they remind me how love can transform people's lives. And connecting with my readers through email, at events and on social media has shown me that you, like Ruby, are busy doing love's work in the world. What an inspiration you are—and what a beautiful difference you make!

We'll be taking another trip to Cedar Ridge soon! In the meantime, I'd love to stay in touch. Head over to www.laurelblountbooks.com and join my beloved group of newsletter subscribers! Every month I share photos, giveaways, behind-the-scenes book news and gotta-try-it recipes. And of course, you can always write me at laureblountwrites@gmail.com.

I look forward to hearing from you!

Much love,
*Laurel*

# Get 3 FREE REWARDS!

**We'll send you 2 FREE Books plus a FREE Mystery Gift.**

**FREE**
Value Over
**$20**

Both the **Love Inspired®** and **Love Inspired® Suspense** series feature compelling novels filled with inspirational romance, faith, forgiveness and hope.

# Get 3 FREE REWARDS!

**We'll send you 2 FREE Books plus a FREE Mystery Gift.**

**FREE** Value Over **$20**

Both the **Harlequin® Special Edition** and **Harlequin® Heartwarming™** series feature compelling novels filled with stories of love and strength where the bonds of friendship, family and community unite.

**YES!** Please send me 2 FREE novels from the Harlequin Special Edition or Harlequin Heartwarming series and my FREE Gift (gift is worth about $10 retail). After receiving them, if I don't wish to receive any more books, I can return the shipping statement marked "cancel." If I don't cancel, I will receive 6 brand-new Harlequin Special Edition books every month and be billed just $5.49 each in the U.S. or $6.24 each in Canada, a savings of at least 12% off the cover price, or 4 brand-new Harlequin Heartwarming Larger-Print books every month and be billed just $6.24 each in the U.S. or $6.74 each in Canada, a savings of at least 19% off the cover price. It's quite a bargain! Shipping and handling is just 50¢ per book in the U.S. and $1.25 per book in Canada.* I understand that accepting the 2 free books and gift places me under no obligation to buy anything. I can always return a shipment and cancel at any time by calling the number below. The free books and gift are mine to keep no matter what I decide.

Choose one:
☐ **Harlequin Special Edition** (235/335 BPA GRMK)

☐ **Harlequin Heartwarming Larger-Print** (161/361 BPA GRMK)

☐ **Or Try Both!** (235/335 & 161/361 BPA GRPZ)

Name (please print)

Address     Apt. #

City     State/Province     Zip/Postal Code

**Email:** Please check this box ☐ if you would like to receive newsletters and promotional emails from Harlequin Enterprises ULC and its affiliates. You can unsubscribe anytime.

## Mail to the **Harlequin Reader Service:**
**IN U.S.A.:** P.O. Box 1341, Buffalo, NY 14240-8531
**IN CANADA:** P.O. Box 603, Fort Erie, Ontario L2A 5X3

**Want to try 2 free books from another series? Call 1-800-873-8635 or visit www.ReaderService.com.**

*Terms and prices subject to change without notice. Prices do not include sales taxes, which will be charged (if applicable) based on your state or country of residence. Canadian residents will be charged applicable taxes. Offer not valid in Quebec. This offer is limited to one order per household. Books received may not be as shown. Not valid for current subscribers to the Harlequin Special Edition or Harlequin Heartwarming series. All orders subject to approval. Credit or debit balances in a customer's account(s) may be offset by any other outstanding balance owed by or to the customer. Please allow 4 to 6 weeks for delivery. Offer available while quantities last.

**Your Privacy**—Your information is being collected by Harlequin Enterprises ULC, operating as Harlequin Reader Service. For a complete summary of the information we collect, how we use this information and to whom it is disclosed, please visit our privacy notice located at corporate.harlequin.com/privacy-notice. From time to time we may also exchange your personal information with reputable third parties. If you wish to opt out of this sharing of your personal information, please visit readerservice.com/consumerschoice or call 1-800-873-8635. **Notice to California Residents**—Under California law, you have specific rights to control and access your data. For more information on these rights and how to exercise them, visit corporate.harlequin.com/california-privacy.

HSEHW23

# COMING NEXT MONTH FROM
## Love Inspired

## THE TEACHER'S CHRISTMAS SECRET
*Seven Amish Sisters* • by Emma Miller

Cora Koffman dreams of being a teacher. But the job is given to newcomer Tobit Lapp instead. When an injury forces the handsome widower to seek out Cora's help, can they get along for the sake of the students? Or will his secret ruin the holidays?

## TRUSTING HER AMISH RIVAL
*Bird-in-Hand Brides* • by Jackie Stef

Shy Leah Fisher runs her own bakery shop in town. When an opportunity to expand her business comes from childhood bully Silas Riehl, she reluctantly agrees to the partnership. They try to keep things professional, but will their past get in the way?

## A COMPANION FOR CHRISTMAS
*K-9 Companions* • by Lee Tobin McClain

When her Christmas wedding gets canceled, first-grade teacher Kelly Walsh takes a house-sitting gig with her therapy dog on the outskirts of town for a much-needed break. Then her late sister's ex-boyfriend, Alec Wilkins, unexpectedly arrives with his toddler daughter, and this holiday refuge could become something more...

## REDEEMING THE COWBOY
*Stone River Ranch* • by Lisa Jordan

After his rodeo career is ruined, cowboy Barrett Stone did not expect to be working with Piper Healy, his late best friend's wife, on his family's ranch. She blames him for her husband's death. Can he prove he's more than the reckless cowboy she used to know?

## FINDING THEIR CHRISTMAS HOME
by Donna Gartshore

Returning home after years abroad, Jenny Powell is eager to spend the holidays with her grandmother at their family home. Then she discovers that old flame David Hart is staying there with his twin girls as well. Could it be the second chance that neither of them knew they needed?

## THEIR SURPRISE SECOND CHANCE
by Lindi Peterson

Widower Adam Hawk is figuring out how to parent his young daughter when an old love, Nicole St. John, returns unexpectedly—with a fully grown child he never knew he had. Nicole needs his help guiding their troubled son. Can they work together for a second chance at family?

---

LICNM0823

# HARLEQUIN
## PLUS

Try the best multimedia subscription service for romance readers like you!

---

## Read, Watch and Play.

Experience the easiest way to get the romance content you crave.

Start your **FREE TRIAL** at
www.harlequinplus.com/freetrial.